# STEP INTO MY WORLD

# STEP INTO MY WORLD

Diana Wynne

Chivers Press  •  G.K. Hall & Co.
Bath, England    Thorndike, Maine USA

SR LH BK
LE HW KM MH AJ VR JM RS VWM JY

This Large Print edition is published by Chivers Press, England, and by G. K. Hall & Co., USA.

Published in 2000 in the U.K. by arrangement with Robert Hale Ltd.

Published in 2000 in the U.S. by arrangement with Robert Hale Ltd.

U.K. Hardcover  ISBN 0-7540-4115-8  (Chivers Large Print)
U.K. Softcover  ISBN 0-7540-4116-6  (Camden Large Print)
U.S. Softcover  ISBN 0-7838-8999-2  (Nightingale Series Edition)

The text of this Large Print edition is unabridged.
Other aspects of the book may vary from the original edition.

Set in 16 pt. New Times Roman.

Printed in Great Britain on acid-free paper.

**British Library Cataloguing in Publication Data available**

**Library of Congress Cataloging-in-Publication Data**

Wynne, Diana, 1928–
    Step into my world / Diana Wynne.
        p.  cm.
    ISBN 0-7838-8999-2 (lg. print : sc : alk. paper)
    1. Women in real estate—Fiction. 2. England—Fiction.
    3. Large type books.  I. Title.
    PR6073.Y69 S74  2000
    823'.914—dc21
                                            00–021442

# CHAPTER ONE

'Blue,' Imogen's romantic Aunt Maude had told her when she was a very little girl, 'is the colour of serenity and happiness. It may also be regal, depending on the shade, for there is a shade of blue to match every mood, every occasion.'

Imogen had been just under five years old at the time of the pronouncement and it had made a deep impression on her young mind as she sat on the bed watching Maude dress to go to the opera.

Indeed Maude looked particularly beautiful that evening. She was a curvaceous little lady and the pale blue satin dress, scattered with pearls, clung to her supple body without a wrinkle. Sapphire and pearl earrings hung from her neat ears and she wore her blond hair in a heavy coronet.

Imogen thought she should have a fur coat, like the one she had seen recently on the television when she was watching an old Fred Astaire and Ginger Rogers film with her mother. Her mother had agreed that it was very beautiful but had added sharply that it was not the sort of coat you could wear to the supermarket.

'You are too little to understand,' Maude said, kissing the top of Imogen's head. 'But

1

you can only get a fur coat by killing a lot of little animals and that is very cruel and unnecessary—see how beautiful this is!' She took a long, blue velvet cloak out of her wardrobe and wrapped it round Imogen. 'There! Isn't that warm and just as glamorous as fur?'

'And as expensive,' Mother snapped. 'Come along now Imogen! Maude's taxi is here and it's time we went home!'

Imogen slid reluctantly off the bed. Even at that age she was aware that her mother was highly critical of Maude's extravagance.

'We'll just have to pray she finds a man wealthy enough to keep her going,' she had said bitterly to her father when Maude had appeared at a family wedding a few weeks earlier looking particularly stunning.

Her father had put his arm round her mother at once and kissed her gently.

'You are still the loveliest of all,' he said. 'And one day we will have so much money that you will be able to have everything you want!' And her mother had smiled back and looked happier but Imogen had not heard her reply because at that moment they had arrived at the church and she was caught up in her well-rehearsed duties as bridesmaid, aware that she was part of the main attraction.

'What a fine big girl!'

'Only four! And she managed so well!'

'Of course she did! She's already a really

dependable person, like her daddy!' Her grandmother had given her a hug and kiss. 'She did everything she had to do very well. She's a great credit to you Elizabeth!' She smiled at Imogen's mother and she had smiled back and she, too, had kissed her and said 'well done' but her attention had really been on Maude, who seemed to have half-a-dozen men around her. Twenty years on, relaxing in her bath with half an hour to spare before she went down to yet another reception, Imogen found she had total recall of both days.

She understood the tensions now and thought wryly that it was just as well her mother did not know at the time that her struggles were only just beginning.

Imogen was only just six when her wonderful, dependable father was killed in a motor accident. Financially things could have been worse. He had left them provided with what appeared to be adequate insurance, but he had not foreseen the rapid rate of inflation ahead, and the real deprivation was simply that he was no longer there.

From time to time other men had called but her mother turned them away. Nobody could measure up to what she had lost. Imogen became her mainstay.

Aunt Maude had been wonderful, discreetly generous. She had found her happiness that night at the opera in the unexpected form of a fifty-year-old banker who had been divorced years before and was reputed never to have looked at another woman since.

'I promise you, Imogen,' Maude told her years later, 'I thought everyone must have noticed the blinding flash between us when we met. He held my hand very gently but we could not let go. I could not believe he was real and later he told me he was afraid I might disappear!'

Imogen had been a bridesmaid again at Maude's wedding, dressed in forget-me-not blue with a wreath of the same tiny blue flowers in her long, blond hair. Once again everything had gone smoothly.

'She will be a great comfort to her poor mother,' someone murmured sympathetically.

'She already is!' her grandmother claimed. 'She is very dependable!'

From that time forward Maude had deferred to her husband in all things and he protected her from all worry. It was not the sort of life the modern woman was supposed to like, Imogen reflected as she wrapped the hotel bathrobe round herself and went back to the bedroom, but sometimes when she was tired she thought how nice it would be to have somebody to lean on. If she could just go down and enjoy the reception tonight because she was not responsible for it!

Finished with her make-up, she climbed carefully into her deep sapphire-blue silk dress, and slid her feet into the matching

4

shoes. It was one of the most successful dresses she had ever had made. A perfect fit, it slenderized her statuesque figure, while its colour stood out amongst many others without being flashy. It was all part of the efficient package she presented to the world and was generally content to do so. So why this evening was she dreaming of Aunt Maude?

She picked up her little gold watch and was about to snap the bracelet onto her wrist when she looked at it again in astonishment. It still said six o'clock, and Imogen's watch simply did not stop!

Years of experience had taught her to pace herself very exactly, but an earlier glance at the same watch had told her she had plenty of time, so she had sat there, doing her make-up slowly, bemused by the fact that she could look so like Maude, but because of her size something quite different was expected of her!

She turned to the clock radio by the bed— 6.27! For the first time ever she was going to be late.

Snatching up her bag she hurried from the room, down the corridor to the lift. It was weirdly quiet on the fourth floor and smelled of paint. The hotel was brand new, purpose-built by the consortium she worked for, and the party this evening was the grand opening. She had been assured that everything was in working order.

She pressed the call button. There was no

5

response. She pressed it again with unusual impatience. This time the lift came slowly into action but decided, apparently on its own initiative, to stop at every floor. She wondered whether to take the stairs, but at that moment it came meekly to a stop in front of her and the doors opened with a gentle sigh. It seemed rude to refuse it, so she stepped in and pressed the button for the first floor.

The lift hesitated.

'Come on!' she said. 'There's never going to be a fifth floor!'

The lift responded with a faint tremor. The lights flickered uncertainly and Imogen wished she had taken the stairs. But they made it to the third floor, stopped, and the doors opened. There was nobody there; presumably the caller had given up as she had so nearly done.

The doors closed again and they continued the descent. All the floor-indicators went out and the lift stopped, though a gentle purring sound indicated there was still life in it.

Imogen was beginning to feel hysterical but she hesitated to press the alarm button. One of the hidden reasons for her efficiency was that she could not bear a fuss of any sort. Pressing the alarm would inevitably cause a fuss. Bells would ring, hall porters would be alerted, engineers called and all the machinery of rescue would be set in motion. It was unnervingly quiet.

She pressed the first floor button again,

stabbing it firmly twice.

This did evoke a response. The lift seemed to rise a few feet, checked, and then fell rapidly, stopped, and the doors opened. Imogen sprang out like a greyhound from a starting trap and set off down the corridor.

The door of the suite was open as she expected and she went in, apologies at the ready. To her surprise there was nobody in the sitting-room and the drinks she had ordered had not been set out. Well, fortunately there was still time to get things put right, but if the management wanted to make a good impression they would have to get things right the first time.

A slight sound from the direction of the bedroom made her turn, beginning to apologize for her lateness as she did so. But the apology choked into a gasp of dismay.

The man who joined her in the sitting-room was definitely not her boss. He was stark naked and rather wet. He carried a glass in one hand while he towelled his hair and beard with the other. Imogen thought the room shook, but he did not seem to be the least perturbed. Putting the glass down he looped the towel deftly round his hips and tucked in the ends.

'I seem to have surprised you,' he said. 'But I was not expecting a visitor!'

'I . . . I'm so sorry! I . . . I . . . seem to be in the wrong suite! I was looking for 104.'

7

'That's all right! I am sure it was a perfectly genuine mistake. You're on the wrong floor. This is 204!' He sounded amused.

Imogen had never felt so confused in her life. If she had ever had an ideal man in mind *this* was he! Mature, with a physique and all-over tan that could only have been developed by hard living in the great outdoors, he had a black velvet voice that hit a responsive chord in her. She was profoundly aware that he was in complete control of this situation as he would be of any other. He was the sort of man to be with in a hijack—and she was too embarrassed to appreciate him.

Grabbing her handbag she made for the door, still apologizing, so she failed to catch his parting words.

Down one floor, the door of 104 was also open, but this time she stopped to check the number and to catch her breath. Here all was well. Don McIntyre sat by the fire with his wife, Jenny, beside him, quietly waiting for their guests.

'You'd best report the lift at once,' he said. 'It can be a harrowing experience to be trapped. Make a note of it on the general report so that we are sure it's seen to!'

'I hope you will find some time to relax this weekend,' Jenny said gently. 'It's not meant to be all work!'

'I enjoy it,' Imogen reminded her, 'and look what we achieve!' They smiled at each other.

In the ten years since Imogen had first come to work for Don they had got to know each other very well, each looking after him in their own way. It had been a small concern, building a few houses here and there, until he met Charles Partindon who had plenty of money and lots of ideas and wanted a builder to carry them out. He seemed to have contacts everywhere. It had been up to Don to sort out the good from the bad.

Jenny kept out of the business now. She saw her role as provider of a solid homebase from which her man could work. But she had a canny way of assessing people and Don brought her to all social meetings knowing that he could trust those on whom she smiled.

It was Jenny who had said Imogen could manage the job when she first came for an interview, who had insisted that she moved with Don when he joined Partindon. It was Jenny who had had the idea for this grand opening so that all the people who had put money and effort into the scheme could come and have a preview.

There was one exception—Arthur Britlore—Sir Arthur Britlore. Imogen had not heard of him before and the reason for his being invited was that he was the great-nephew of old Mrs Enderby, who had invested the money to get Don started in the first place, and received a handsome return on her investment.

'They tell me Sir Arthur has arrived,' Don said, as though picking up her thought. 'He doesn't know anyone apart from Mrs E. of course, so see that he gets to know the others.'

At that moment Charles Partindon and his wife arrived. The party began to gather; their greetings and small talk were all very predictable.

Roy Lavers arrived, immaculate as ever and giving the impression he was much more important than he was. Actually he was not a member of the firm at all, but a very good supplier. After an initial skirmish Imogen learnt to accept his help while keeping him at arm's length, and he had settled into the happy, purely working relationship she had with all the men she met.

He had given up trying to seduce her, treated her with friendly consideration and frequently asked for information. She was friendly, accepted his help and gave him such information as it was desirable, from Don's point of view, that he should have.

'Who,' he asked now, coming straight to the point, 'is Sir Arthur, and how does he fit in here?'

'Except that he is related to Mrs Enderby and is escorting her I really don't know,' Imogen replied.

Roy's eyebrows rose. It was not like Imogen to fail to do her homework.

'I don't think he needs us particularly,' he

10

said. 'He has an estate in Leicestershire and he drives a special Bentley—vintage not veteran—but expensive.'

Imogen smiled. She was very familiar with Roy's technique of supplying a little, often irrelevant, information to coax a reciprocation from his listener. She knew about the estate in Leicestershire and also about the mining interests in Australia . . . Australia! That suntan! The man in 204! What was it he had called after her? See you round? See you later? She was sure now that it was 'See you . . .!' Oh, surely the man in 204 could not be their mystery guest?

She felt herself flush, then pale. Roy was looking at her curiously

'Are you all right?' he asked.

'A bit tired. Nothing dinner won't put right!' she lied. 'Is everybody else here now?'

She looked round the room. Don was talking to the chief accountant and Geoff Broadbent, who looked after their international accounts, while their wives chatted to Jenny. Every now and then Geoff treated Imogen to a cool stare, which always amused her. He had never forgiven her for turning down his offer of becoming his personal assistant, and possibly something more. He had had two secretaries and two mistresses since and was aware of Imogen's dislike in spite of her unfailing civility whenever they met.

11

'Just two more to come,' she said, as the door opened and Mrs Enderby made her entrance on the arm of Sir Arthur Britlore— the man from 204. Never a large lady, Mrs Enderby had aged down into a humming-bird. She loved floating clothes in brilliant colours and always had a silk shawl wrapped round her shoulders. This evening she was easily the oldest lady in the room and she was escorted by the most handsome man. She was unashamedly delighted as she led him over to Jenny.

With a thudding heart Imogen walked slowly across the room to meet them. Mrs Enderby was more than just a board member, she was a friend and Imogen bent to receive her little kiss of greeting.

'And this is my nephew, Arthur Britlore,' Mrs Enderby's voice was warm with pride. 'Arthur, here is Imogen, Don's right hand!'

Arthur was completely at ease, his whole demeanour registering only polite attentiveness to an introduction. Imogen had never realized before that dark brown eyes could be so cool. They exchanged well-worn phrases of greeting and Imogen moved away to get them a drink feeling rejected. She had certainly not wanted a public acknowledgement of their earlier meeting but such total lack of recognition was unnerving.

'But to be introduced as someone's right hand is hardly enlivening,' she thought ruefully as she poured their drinks. 'Am I really just part of the furniture, the speaking bit of the telephone or the computer, or an unthinking extension of Don?' Clearly, if the room had rocked, it had been only for her!

She watched the evening going as planned. There was no need to worry about Arthur. Everyone was so eager to meet him that he circulated without any intervention from her.

Dinner was excellent and after coffee the guests moved on to the ballroom or games-room to meet others who had been asked to the opening but were not members of the charmed inner circle. Glancing at her watch soon after eleven, Imogen wondered if the party would ever end.

It seemed desperately hot and noisy in the ballroom. Her head was throbbing and she craved air. Using the excuse that she must go to the telex room to check whether there were any incoming messages, she managed to get a few moments on her own.

Earlier she had seen a small sign, 'Gardens', and she wondered if the door was open and the gardens finished yet.

The passage was brightly lit and to her joy the door at the end yielded to her touch. She went out onto a wide, paved terrace from which a flight of stone steps curved down to a floodlit sunken garden. Paved walks wound between small rockeries to meet again at the far end at a lily pond, fed by an artificial waterfall with a group of three children and a dog playing at its foot. Not great art, perhaps, but there was a liveliness about the little stone figures that appealed to her.

It was too cold to stay out for long, but for a moment it was refreshing to breathe the sharp air and to wonder if she really could detect anything of the wild spirit of the Brontë country that lay not so far beyond the town.

A faint sound behind her made her realize she was not alone and she spun round in alarm.

'I'm sorry. I did not mean to frighten you. I needed space!' That voice again. Imogen steadied herself against the cold stone balustrade as Arthur came towards her out of the shadows. 'I hoped for a glimpse of the night sky and the stars,' he went on easily, 'but the lighting drowns everything above it and it's cloudy anyway.'

'I was wondering about the moors,' Imogen replied. 'But this will be another trip when I shall not see further than the hotel!' She was annoyed to hear a faint trace of bitterness in her voice. Conferences, exhibitions, development sites absorbed her travelling time and energy and one hotel room was very like another . . .

'Do you have to dash back tomorrow?' The question sounded casual and Imogen was not sure how to answer.

'We were going to drive back after lunch,'

14

she said.

'My aunt does not like driving. She would prefer to go by train, even on a Sunday! Would you let me drive you home and take in a little of the country on the way?'

'That's a very nice idea. Thank you!' she said suppressing her immediate question—what does he want to know? She was too used to men asking her out to lunch or dinner because she held some information they could use.

'Then let's start as early as we can.' He made it sound a matter of convenience and could not know how her heartbeat had quickened.

'I should be free by twelve,' she said.

'That's fine.'

She made her way back to the party via the telex room. There were a couple of messages sent to show the system worked.

For the rest of the evening she played out her role as Don's right hand. She also learned why he was so anxious that Arthur should be well treated. Mrs Enderby was enjoying a little power game of her own, making her will.

'It's not that Arthur needs anything,' she said in a low voice to Imogen as they sat together in the ballroom and the blare of the music effectively prevented anybody overhearing them. 'With what he has inherited already and what he has made out of that he has more than enough, so, I could simply leave

15

my entire holding back to Don, but then he would still be alone and I feel that sometimes he might like support. So now I have introduced them and we shall have to see what Arthur thinks about it!'

Imogen agreed that Sir Arthur would be a wonderful ally, for which observation she received a brilliant smile and a pat on the hand and they changed the conversation. But watching him as he moved from group to group, Imogen wondered what Arthur's assessment was. He was not the sort of man to submit quietly to being vetted and he could refuse to join them. Meanwhile she observed with amusement that there was quite fierce competition amongst the ladies for his attention.

It was after one o'clock before the party began to slow down, and closer to two before Jenny came to thank her for all she had done.

'You make it appear so effortless, my dear,' she said. 'But we do appreciate it.'

Imogen went slowly up the four flights of stairs to her room alone, with the usual feelings of relief and deflation after such an evening. But this time there was tomorrow, or rather today, to look forward to. She stood for a minute or two under a cool shower and then, still naked, she brushed out her hair, revelling in the caress of the air on her body, the freedom of being without clothes.

In room 204 Arthur lay completely relaxed

16

in his bed, sound asleep, breathing gently, at peace with the world.

Below him in 104 Jenny waited patiently for her husband to finish his nightly bend and stretch. When he got into bed she curled up against him as usual in the safety of his arm, her head on his shoulder.

'I think,' she said, 'you are going to lose Imogen.'

'Why? Who's trying to poach her now?' He was used to other men offering Imogen more to come and work for them and adjusted her salary accordingly.

'Arthur Britlore.'

'Why does he need a secretary all of a sudden?'

'Not as a secretary, duffer! As a wife!'

'Huh?' For once Don was shaken. 'What are you on about, woman? She has been giving men what I believe is known as the frozen mitt for years, and they didn't take any notice of each other all evening apart from one sort of courtesy twirl round the dance floor!'

'Did they not?' Jenny laughed softly and kissed the corner of his mouth. 'He hardly took his eyes off her and she was like an overwound clock. At some convenient time tomorrow she will tell you she is not driving home with us. Sir Arthur is driving her!'

'Oh!' Don was not going to argue but he did not believe her.

# CHAPTER TWO

Rain had fallen during the night and was still falling when Imogen drew back her curtains. Not a day for viewing the wilds of Yorkshire in comfort.

Anticipation, she had been taught, was the key to efficiency, but she could scarcely have anticipated this invitation. She sorted decisively through the few clothes she had with her and found she could muster a pair of low-heeled shoes and plain tights that went well with the pleated skirt she had travelled up in. She could pack the jacket that went with the skirt, wear a jumper over her blouse and carry her coat.

Having made up her mind she showered and dressed, brushed her hair till it shone, and decided to leave it loose. She packed neatly and swiftly, and ran downstairs to find an early breakfast.

To her surprise she met Geoff Broadbent in the foyer, clad in a track suit and puffing after an early morning run. She thought he looked finished rather than fit.

'Not a very nice morning for running!' she said brightly as he glared at her. Then she smiled to herself as she remembered his wife was with him and he was having to make all the accounts of his weekends away seem true.

He always said he had a run every day. 'Ah! There's Roy!' she was able to smile openly now. 'We're both early risers so we generally have breakfast together.'

'Then you might apply some of that great efficiency of yours to getting the lift fixed,' Geoff said sourly as he pushed past her and made for the stairs.

'What have you done to upset him?' Roy asked as they made their way to the dining-room.

'I don't have to do anything,' Imogen replied. 'He only has to see me to be irritable.'

'Ah, well! What about today? Are you free to do anything?'

'Not really. Arthur Britlore is driving me home and we are going to see a bit of the country on the way—weather permitting.'

'Don't you ever stop working!' Roy frowned. 'I would have thought after getting this place off the ground you deserved a day off.'

'That was how I saw it,' Imogen replied gently, suddenly annoyed that Roy could only see her in a working relationship with a man. 'Though he may well be right,' she thought. 'Perhaps all Arthur wants is information.'

An hour later Don found her in the little secretarial office off the conference room finishing off the report of the weekend.

'You did not have to do that today,' he said. 'Monday would have done!'

'Monday is always very busy.'

'But you've got an assistant now, to take over the donkey work and give you more time for this sort of thing,' he said testily. taking the file to a chair by the window to read it.

Imogen felt her mouth tighten. They were on tricky ground. It was Jenny who had noticed on one of her rare visits to the office that Imogen's workload had increased tremendously as the scope of the business widened, but that a lot that she did could be handled by any competent shorthand typist, blessed with discretion, as some of the information they gathered was commercially sensitive.

Imogen was grateful for the suggestion and knew just whom she wanted to help her, and that was when the trouble started. She had made one of her rare errors and assumed that as whoever came was to be her assistant she would be allowed to choose which girl she wanted from the general secretarial office, and she wanted Cathy.

But Cathy was not overwhelmingly attractive. If you bothered to look you would see the continual good humour which lit her eyes and notice that she had lovely, beautifully kept hands, but very few people got past noticing that she was overweight and gallumphed rather than walked across the office. Apparently lodged in the typing pool on a comparatively low salary for ever her clothes were generally dull. But Imogen had happened to meet her outside the office several times in unexpected places like art galleries and the theatre and knew that she could look quite different and had a good dress sense. More importantly Cathy was quick and absolutely accurate in her work.

So she had asked for Cathy and been told that even if the choice had been hers, which it was not, she ought to be able to see what a totally unsuitable person Cathy was. Imogen kept her anger in check but pleaded her cause in vain and for the first time Don refused to support her. Mrs Simmons, the Personnel manager, saw her point but did not think moving Cathy to the executive floor would transform her sufficiently even with Imogen's guidance. They had chosen Annette; curvaceous, vivacious Annette, who undoubtedly added sparkle to the office and was not immune to male flattery.

'Immaculate, as usual,' Don handed the file back to her with a smile. 'But Annette could have typed it up from your notes. You must see that she does her fair share of the work!'

'There's plenty for her to do,' Imogen returned the smile and kept her voice even. 'Or has she complained?'

They were fencing now; something they had never done before. But the morning Annette had been appointed Broadbent had deliberately spoken by the door to Don's office so that Imogen would overhear.

'Well thank goodness that's settled then,' he

said. 'A headmistress and a hephalump in the same office would be too much! And if I hear that Miss Gordon has been putting that little girl down unfairly she will have me to answer to. Once they think they are on the shelf these older women get so bitchy.'

Don's reply had been brief and inaudible and they had ignored the incident. In fact Annette's presence had enlivened the office. She was an intelligent, willing little worker, delighted with her promotion, but there was a subtle change in Don's and Imogen's relationship.

'I have been offered a 'day off' today!' Imogen said. 'Sir Arthur has offered to drive me home and show me a little of Yorkshire on the way—if that is all right.' She was clearing the desk and covering the typewriter as she spoke, but he took so long to reply that she turned to look at him, wondering if he had heard her.

'Of course . . . of course it's all right—after all it is Sunday! See you tomorrow!' He went off looking quite startled.

She took her keys back to Reception and met Arthur. He was carrying a rather damp Burberry and umbrella.

'Well, I got my aunt safely onto the train from Leeds,' he said smiling at her. 'How are you fixed?'

'All set,' Imogen replied, her heart suddenly lighter. She was going to forget all about

Partindon Associates, she decided, and just enjoy the day.

'Then let's have a civilized drink and a light lunch in the salad bar and be on our way.'

The Bentley was magnificent and smelled of freshly cleaned leather. She admired it unstintingly. He clipped the seatbelt round her and offered her a knee rug.

'No radio!' he said as they purred smoothly out of the car park. 'I could have one fitted but it would be an anachronism. My aunt would certainly not approve!'

'It would spoil everything,' Imogen said. 'Radios are intrusive.' She gazed out at the wet countryside. They were completely isolated from the world now, cut off by the steady sound of the motor and the gentle slap of the windscreen wipers and even more protected by the falling rain, yet they were not entirely at ease.

She found herself waiting for the first comment, friendly of course, about the weekend, or the people at the weekend, that would start them talking about Partindon's. She did not know what Arthur was waiting for, so, deliberately, she turned her thoughts away.

She thought instead how Maude would love a journey in a car like this with such an escort, and suddenly she decided that she would be Maude for the day. She would stop being the efficient Miss Gordon, five foot nine inches tall, ten-and-a-half stone and well able

23

to look after herself and everybody else. She would be a regal five foot three, expecting to be waited on, ready to be entertained but not organizing anything.

'I thought we should change our plans a bit,' Arthur said. 'This is no weather for the hills and dales and we are certainly not equipped for it. Suppose we go to Ripon and have a look round and then if it stops raining we can visit Fountains Abbey before we turn south.'

'That sounds lovely.' Imogen smiled happily, and settled into her new role. 'You must miss the Australian sunshine!'

'It does rain in some parts of Australia too, you know! We even have some dry stone walls out there, just like the ones here!' He nodded at the fields they were passing. 'When the original settlers went there they took their crafts with them and in the Kiama district of New South Wales a man called Thomas Newing built miles and miles of dry stone walls. They'll stand the test of time as well as these have.

'What I really miss is the space in the outback—space all round me and such a lot of sky. Some people hate it; not just because they are lonely but because there are not enough walls and buildings to bring space down to size.' He glanced at her speculatively. 'Have you lived in the country?'

'No . . . no, I have never lived outside a town,' she admitted. 'Nor even spent a holiday in the country,' she thought to herself. As children they had gone to the seaside at Bournemouth for their holidays; later there had been school trips, then package tours abroad. The country was the bit you drove through between one town and another unless you visited a stately home or some specific beauty spot.

'Tell me about Australia—your ranch,' Imogen invited. He looked so completely at home behind the wheel of the Bentley, confident of his driving and of the route he was taking, that it would be easy to accept that he was in his usual setting. But sitting close to him Imogen was aware of the energy of the man and could easily imagine him riding alone through rough country or sailing single-handed round the world.

'Ah! That is a different world,' he said smiling at her. 'It even seems to be in a different time. Sometimes when I am there I feel guilty. I wonder if I should be enjoying so much freedom and leaving everything in England to look after itself. Yet I am not really free out there. I am as much tied to the land I own as my fathers were to the place in Leicestershire. It all has to be cared for—but not developed in quite the way your people see development!' He spoke lightly but Imogen wondered if he was trying to say that he did not think very highly of Partindon's.

She was saved the trouble of replying by

their arrival in Ripon. He drove slowly through the old, narrow streets, up round the massive front of the cathedral to park the car. The rain had eased off and walking did not seem too impossible.

'I think we can manage with one umbrella,' he said. He held it open so that she was sheltered as soon as she left the car and keeping close together they walked swiftly up through the park and crossed the road to the great, iron studded west door. Once inside the cathedral he found a place for the wet umbrella and returned to her side.

Here the spirit of peace and worship was tangible. There was no service in progress so they were able to wander round quietly as they wished. They walked together up the great nave and stood at the crossing to look up into the tower, supported by two round and two perpendicular arches.

'Why are they different?' Imogen asked.

'Trouble with the planning committee!' Arthur replied solemnly.

'Be serious!'

'I am!' he said. 'There was a small earthquake in the middle of the fifteenth century and part of the tower collapsed. The restorers built new pointed arches to match the new nave and planned to take away the other two round arches and finish with four pointed ones. But even in those days there was the red tape to get through, and probably a cash problem. The church commissioners said 'no' and they just had to leave it like that! Come and look at the wood carvings.' He led her up to the choir stalls to look at the wonderfully carved seats.

It seemed that every carver had been given a free hand to carve as he wished. By now Imogen had found her way into the little guidebook a lady had offered her as they came in. She found the list of the carvings surprising. Flowers and fruit she might have suggested if she had been asked what subjects she expected the craftsmen to choose; but two pigs dancing to bagpipes and a mermaid with a mirror seemed slightly bizarre.

She moved slowly from one to the next, entranced by their liveliness, and paused by the only saintly relief.

'Who was St Cuthman?' she asked. 'And why did he have to push his mother eastwards in a barrow? It must have been a very charitable act or he would not have been made a saint!'

'I don't really know why he has his picture here,' Arthur admitted, 'unless it was because he was a shepherd and this is a great sheep county. He lived down in the South-west, and when his father died he and his poor old mother were evicted from their home. She was too frail to walk so he built a cart to carry her and set off eastwards to find work and a new home. When they were able to settle again he built a church as a thank offering. There's a rather nice play about it.'

'Uhm!' Imogen regarded him thoughtfully. 'You know a lot of interesting things.'

'Sign of an idle youth I fear!' he smiled. 'Too much time to spend on impractical things like reading and finding out.'

'But you are not impractical,' she thought. She had seen well-muscled bodies such as his on the building and development sites and his hands, well-kept and well-manicured as they were, were strong and used.

They finished their tour, descending the narrow winding stair to the crypt where the stone floors and walls had been worn smooth by many passing pilgrims. Then out again through the west door to find that the rain had stopped.

'We may not get another chance to stretch our legs,' Arthur said. So they walked briskly up to the market place to look at the outside of the Wakeman's House.

'I believe the Wakeman still blows his horn at nine o'clock each evening as he used to to settle the city for the night. You can hear it three miles away at Fountains. But they also warn you not to put all your faith in the Wakeman!'—and he pointed to the city motto, picked out in gold, at the top of the council house.

'Except ye Lord keep ye cittie ye Wakeman waketh in vain.'

'Yes! We do rather think that we can do it all ourselves these days, don't we,' Imogen said, 'in spite of frequent reminders that we can't!'

The narrow, twisting country roads to Fountains Abbey forced them to drive slowly. Imogen had expected to see it from some way off, but in fact the site the monks had chosen at the head of a secluded valley was well hidden from the world. There were not many visitors on such a wet and wintry Sunday afternoon, so they were able to wander peacefully through the ruins.

There were no great steel supports here, Imogen noted, yet the monks had managed to build a graceful spiral stairway in the wall of the tower, and a few minutes later she stood entranced by the geometric precision of the vaulting of the refectory roof.

'And we think we're so clever to put up the buildings we design!' she said.

'Techniques keep changing,' Arthur said. 'We have to do our best with the materials at hand. We would have the most enormous quarries if we used stone for all our building today.'

'But our buildings never make graceful ruins,' she replied, thinking of the tortured, masses of twisted steel and concrete on the demolition sites. 'Stone was taken from here to build other houses—we are just left with a heap of rubble that is often difficult to dispose of.

Already the winter evening was drawing in but they walked a short way down by the water. Away from the little weir the river ran silently but a slight breeze rustled through the trees and shrubs and whispered its own message to the long grass. When they turned to look back at the Abbey and the great tower which still stood at nearly a hundred and sixty feet, Imogen felt the rain again falling gently on her upturned face.

'We'd better get back to the car,' Arthur said, leading the way up to the main path. At the top of the slope two women were standing huddled together, looking about them.

'Peaceful, isn't it?' one said.

'Very quiet,' the other agreed. They sounded faintly uneasy as though the unwonted quiet was too much for them. Imogen waited until they were out of earshot then she laughed.

'I'll bet it wasn't quiet when they were building it,' she said. 'Can't you imagine it? All that stone being delivered and cut and heaved into place with the foreman shouting orders, and everybody getting hungry and tired and the cooks moaning because the firewood was damp!'

'Indeed, at one time the local wild life and such peasants as might have been round must have thought it was more peaceful in the scrublands before the monks got started. But they made it habitable and productive and more beautiful, which was a great achievement.' He unlocked the car and settled her into the passenger seat.

She found that she really enjoyed playing at being Aunt Maude and being fussed over a bit as he tucked the knee rug round her until the car warmed up. She waited until he had negotiated the turn out of the carpark and they were back on the open road before she spoke again.

'You are very fond of England, aren't you, and you have land of your own, so why did you go to Australia? Did you feel you had run out of space here?'

For a moment he did not reply and she wondered if she had been lulled by the intimacy of the car and the rain to become too personal.

'No,' he replied slowly, 'I don't think I realized how much the space mattered to me until I had experienced it. I went to Australia for the oldest reason in the world—a woman!' He laughed, but there was a slightly bitter note to it.

'I'm sorry! I shouldn't have asked!'

'Oh! It was a long time ago and I should be over it now. I had loved her since we were children, but she married somebody else and then they were both killed in a motor crash. I felt I wanted a complete change of scene, a different life. We already had property in Australia but some of it was difficult territory

31

and not much was being done about it. It was a challenge and out there I could be a different person—no background, no title! They generally call me "Art"!'

'And you succeeded?'

'Once we got the water problem solved it was not so difficult. I must just get round to building a proper house now.'

'Then would Australia be your real home—would you give up England altogether?'

They were joining the A1 and for a moment or two he concentrated wholly on working his way into the fast-moving traffic. Imogen felt warm and secure. She slid a little lower in her seat and rested her head. She had not realized how tired she was.

'I hope I will never have to give up the place in Leicestershire,' Arthur said. 'I have not been there for years now and Aunt Enderby says it needs a lot of attention. I shall have to see to it while I am in England this time.'

He was silent again, apparently giving his whole attention to the traffic, and she was content to sit quietly beside him.

'Time for dinner!' he said, 'before we get any closer to London,' and he took the next turn off the motorway. 'I hope you are as hungry as I am!' A few moments later he stopped outside a small country hotel. There were cars parked in what had once been a stable-yard and light glowed invitingly from the windows.

The candle-lit tables were sheltered by high settle seating and the steady patter of the rain on the window intensified the warmth and security of the room. She was rested now and all the emotions that had been dulled by fatigue were waking, unfurling within her like exotic orchids, vibrantly eager for sunshine and life. In all her twenty-six years she had never so longed to be close to any man as she wanted to be close to Arthur now.

'What a lovely place,' she said. 'Did you know about it or did you find it quite by chance?'

'By chance!' he said gaily, and she looked at him with genuine admiration.

'Then I hope you realize,' she said, 'that to find somewhere like this, able to take you in for a meal, without a reservation, on a Sunday evening in the winter is as lucky as finding a water-hole in the desert, if not luckier!'

'Ah! I don't leave that to chance!' he said, but he laughed and they started their meal on a lighthearted note that she did not dare to try to alter and with which he seemed content. She did wonder, for a moment, after her second glass of wine, what his reaction would be if she suggested that they did not go any further, and stayed the night. But that was not what she really wanted.

'We'd better be on our way!' he said when they had had coffee by the fire and reluctantly she agreed with him. Perhaps they were

33

destined to be just good friends, or maybe there was someone in Australia he had not mentioned. The thought sobered her as the cold night air hit them.

## CHAPTER THREE

Imogen did not sleep well.

She had persuaded Arthur that she would be perfectly safe if he put her into a taxi outside Euston station. It would save him an awkward drive through north London to her flat, and she was thankful when he agreed.

She had let herself in quietly and closing the door had, for a moment, leaned her back against it and savoured the relief of being alone as usual. Being on her own was familiar; but it had been a long time since she had been alone for the greater part of the day with one other person, let alone a man whose attitude to her was so ambivalent but whose company could rouse such emotion in her. She was tired.

Her only brush with love had been when she was fifteen. She had conceived a hopeless passion for Jeremy Hawkins, the local swimming club diving champion. Swimming was the only sport she enjoyed, but she had joined the diving class just to be near him, and for a while they seemed to make progress.

Nobody ever knew what it cost her, how much courage it had taken, to force herself to make those first dives.

She had dived, and dived, practising with furious concentration to earn a place in his class and had won a place in the team. Life-saving was compulsory and because she was so much larger than the boys her age she was paired off with Jeremy and their physical contact delighted her. Because they lived in the same direction from the pool he took to calling for her on practice nights and walked home with her afterwards.

But then came the day when her ears hurt, she felt sick and giddy after their swimming session. The doctor was kind, but definite—diving was to stop altogether and so was swimming for the time being.

'Oh, Porky! I am sorry!' Jeremy was completely genuine and sincere. In fact it was his very affection for her that caused him to make the slip, but the nickname hit her like a slap in the face and she burst into tears. He comforted her as best he could, awkwardly trying to dry her tears with his swimming towel, never realizing their immediate cause. 'I'll have to go,' he said. 'I'll be late for practice but I'll see you round.'

And he had seen her, talked to her when they met and asked what she was doing and called her Imogen. It seemed soon after that he had started going steady with a wand of a girl.

Imogen had regarded herself long and hard in the mirror and gritted her teeth. Never, never again, she vowed, would anybody call her 'Porky'! She brought all her powers of determination to one point—her appearance. Nothing would ever make her petite, but slender, elegant and well-dressed she would be whatever it cost. Her private triumph came the day she was spotted by a model-agency talent scout and turned the offer down.

Now self-discipline forced her to unpack, put everything away and lay out her clothes for the morning, but her mind was reviving all the sweetness and urgency of that young love for Jeremy. He had witnessed but never really recognized her metamorphosis, being too preoccupied with his own growing up. Soon after her career had taken her away from home, he had married and she lost touch with him.

Now, she wondered, what had she turned herself into? Did every man find her completely unapproachable?

She turned the pillows again and again and dreamed of Arthur, ridiculously attired with corks bobbing round his broadbrimmed hat, riding away from her in a cloud of dust into an alien land.

'I am totally ignorant of everything that makes up his life,' she thought dismally and giving up all idea of sleep she turned off the alarm clock and got up. She was left with rather more time than usual to walk to the office.

Arriving was always a pleasure. Bob Shaw, the security guard, opened the big glass door for her with his usual cheerful grin. He was a short, bulky man, a retired Marine Commando, and she had once asked him how he enjoyed this life of comparative inactivity after the excitement of his service.

'The only skill I was really taught was how to kill,' he said,' and I'm just happy I stayed alive. If you'd asked me years ago I don't believe I would have said I was looking forward to a change, but now I reckon I see more of the world by standing here and letting it go round me than I ever saw crawling through some rotten jungle!' But he remained a careful man.

'There was a man asking for you on the phone very early this morning,' he told her. 'Sir Arthur Brit something he said. He wanted to know if I had your home telephone number. But I wasn't sure . . . so I said he would have to wait until somebody from Personnel got here, or I could pass a message when you came in. Was that all right?'

'Perfect, thank you! I left very early in any case, so he would probably have missed me.' She went swiftly up in the lift to her office, her heart beating a little faster than usual.

The messages Annette had taken on Friday

37

were neatly written on the memo pad, the filing done and a small pile of letters was waiting for her approval. The child seemed to have managed very well. Opening her briefcase and taking out the papers, Imogen began her day's work. By the time Annette arrived, sparkling and slightly breathless, she was well into her stride.

At nine o'clock her private telephone rang. Instinct told her to count to ten, slowly, and Annette looked at her in surprise and asked if she should take it, but Imogen smiled and shook her head, she had savoured the moment long enough—and she could be wrong.

'Good morning! Imogen Gordon speaking.'

'Good morning to you!' His voice was gentle, almost caressing. 'I tried to get your number earlier but your security man was well trained.'

'Nothing personal I assure you!'

'I know! I should have taken your number last night. I've been feeling guilty about letting you go home alone at that time of night, and then not knowing how you got to the office or at what time!'

'Well, I got home safely, thank you!' Imogen laughed. 'And I walked here safely this morning after an early start.' She could not remember anyone ever having wondered how she got to the office, as long as she got there. 'And thank you for a very nice day yesterday.' It was inadequate but she did not feel she could say anything more with Annette listening in. Perhaps he sensed the difficulty as his voice became more formal.

'I had hoped to take you to lunch one day,' he said, 'but something has cropped up,' and she wondered if this was a gentle brush-off, 'but I'll ring you before the end of the week— all right?'

'Lovely! Thank you!' The line went dead.

She replaced her receiver slowly. He still had not asked for her home number and she did not think he was usually so forgetful.

'Here is my report of the opening,' she said to Annette. 'You can read it through and you will know almost as much about it as if you had been there! Then would you please send copies to the "A" circulation list and put one on the microfile.' They were back to business again.

The day went smoothly enough though Don seemed very curious to know about her trip south with Sir Arthur. He always enquired if she had had a pleasant weekend or a good holiday but unless she chose to give him many details he never pushed her for information.

'Does Mrs Enderby really think she needs to make her will so secure just yet?' Imogen decided to ask as few questions herself. 'She seems to be in very good form!'

'Ah! She's a very sensible woman,' Don replied. 'Not the least bit afraid to acknowledge the fact that she is old. She just

39

wants to get everything settled, then she can relax and enjoy what time she has left—and she plans on enjoying it!'

Imogen returned to her own office to find Roy flirting with Annette, who was enjoying the attention. As usual he had an almost valid reason for being there.

'I know these can go straight to Broadbent's office,' he said waving a large envelope, 'but I just called in to see how you were.'

'We're fine, thanks—and busy!' Imogen smiled. There was an easy-going charm about the man that could not be denied even though she knew it should not be trusted.

'I can take a hint!' He stood up easily, resettling his jacket with a slight shrug of his shoulders. 'Be seeing you!'

Annette watched him go, her eyes lingering for a moment on the closed door. Imogen thought it worth another warning.

'Don't take him seriously, Annette,' she said. 'He's been divorced twice and has a bad track record where girls are concerned. He comes in here mainly to learn what's going on. Anything he needs to know gets sent to him officially, so however irrelevant it may seem keep all information to yourself and him at arm's length!' She spoke lightly but Annette looked resentful and Geoff Broadbent came in as she finished speaking. Undoubtedly he had met Roy in the corridor and guessed of whom she was speaking. He glanced from one girl to the other.

'You can't expect to have all the attention now,' he said waspishly to Imogen. 'Are you all right Annette? You seem to have managed very well last week when we were all away.' He smiled fondly at the younger girl who responded with a slightly breathless,

'Everything's fine, thank you, Mr Broadbent!'

'You stirrer!' Imogen thought, while aloud she said pleasantly, 'Good morning, Geoff! Don is waiting for you!'

The day was nearly over when Bob Shaw came to the office with a small packet addressed to her personally on a bookshop label.

'A messenger boy brought it in,' Bob said, 'and as I was just going off duty I thought I would bring it up in case they missed you on your way out.'

It was a copy of *The Boy With A Cart* by Christopher Fry with a card enclosed:

'Here is the story behind the carving that you were curious about,' the writing was neat and strong, 'the story of a young lad who was not afraid to take his skill to new places when times changed and to learn different ones. I hope you will enjoy it—I am going to Leics. to open up the old homestead. Please come down with Don and Jenny for the day on Sunday. Jenny will arrange it with you. Yrs—A.B.'

It was hardly a love-letter yet her heart was

41

singing. If he had felt the need to send anything there were so many conventional gifts, flowers, chocolates, he could have sent, but this showed thoughtful remembrance. For a moment she smoothed the book between the palms of her hands then she slipped it back into the envelope in which it had arrived. She could hardly wait to get home.

Bob and Annette were looking at her curiously, but she could think of no explanation for them other than to thank Bob for bringing her the packet. Walking home she was walking on air as though Arthur were waiting for her. When she got in she put the book by her bed determined to wait until she could relax and enjoy reading it.

While she cooked a meal and got ready for bed she was going over again the time she had spent with him, and every now and then, unbidden, the vivid memory of their first meeting would flash into her mind. Each time she snapped it off like an unwanted light but the image of him remained just behind her eyes and would not be extinguished.

Deliberately she piled up the pillows and settled herself to read the play, set in a peaceful, rural England when life moved at foot pace and Cuthman's only means of transport was a hand-cart. It was a gently humorous, sensitive story moving with love from tragedy to the miraculous completion of the church at Steyning and Imogen could see it all as she read slowly, savouring the scenes.

For some time after she had finished she lay with the book between her hands wondering about the man who had sent it. She felt she was getting to know a different man to the one she had been expecting to meet. The man who had sent this book was not the aloof, astute, boardroom magnate he was supposed to be, and she doubted that any of his Australian colleagues who roughed it with him in the outback would even know that such books existed.

She could understand why the story of Cuthman appealed to him. They had a lot in common, both hit by tragedy that left them little choice but to move on, somewhere. Cuthman had had to take his mother along and she had trusted him .

'And I would trust Arthur too, anywhere,' Imogen thought dreamily as she switched off the light and sank dreamily into the pillows, into his arms . . .

Jenny rang her early the next day about the invitation to Leicestershire, arranging where to meet her . It was just as well Annette was in the office as Imogen took an unusual time to write a note of thanks to Arthur and overspent her lunch hour looking at clothes. As she turned in front of the fitting-room mirrors she imagined Arthur was with her and over her shoulder she looked for approval in his dark eyes.

43

'Lunch,' she said to the sales girl, 'lunch in the country on Sunday . . . rather formal I think and staying on into the evening for an early meal before we drive back to town.'

The girl smiled. She might not have got the whole picture but she recognized love when she saw it, and produced a dress in soft, blue wool, a swinging tweed coat a shade darker and a silk scarf.

'There!' she said standing back to allow Imogen to get an all-round view. 'Fairly plain shoes would be best and a large bag so you can take everything to freshen up easily. Would you like to see some shoes while you have got the coat on?'

Imogen was aware that she was being swept along but did not care. She signed a three-figure cheque without a qualm and left the shop with the outfit complete.

Annette was openly curious and full of admiration. 'You are so lucky to be tall,' she said. 'I could never wear a coat like that. It would drown me!'

Sunday dawned clear and calm and Don drove them swiftly out of London to the wide, green county of Leicestershire. The 'old homestead' as Arthur had called it was not in fact particularly old but a large, solid Victorian house, built for a big, wealthy family with a retinue of servants.

Arthur greeted them on the stone steps that rose to a massive front door and led them

44

inside to where a huge coke stove blazed a warm welcome. Oil paintings in heavy gilt frames hung round the hall and up the walls of the wide, polished wood staircase.

'I am so glad you could come,' he said as he took their coats. 'The house feels very unlived-in, but now you can help me wake it up.' For a moment he looked at her and Imogen thought he approved of what he saw but he was already leading them into the next room.

'Some of my neighbours have joined us for a drink before lunch,' he said. 'Aunt Enderby is acting as hostess!'

Imogen had the extraordinary feeling that she had stepped back in time or onto a stage set. Great log fires burned at each end of the room, and two large yellow labradors sprawled on the hearth rug before one of them. Six elegant windows with long velvet curtains down one wall looked out onto a paved rose garden. Many more paintings hung on the darkly papered walls and the room was furnished with heavy, brocade-covered sofas and chairs.

Their entrance caused a pause in the general conversation and Mrs Enderby detatched herself from one group and fluttered over to meet them.

'Come in, come in!' she said. 'Now you must' meet our friends.' They listened politely to the introductions and were friendly but Imogen was aware that they, Don, Jenny and herself

45

were on the outside of the circle. These were the county country folk, who talked of country matters. It was not that they were aggressively horsey, they were not, but their lives had a totally different quality and meaning to hers and they sensed, without having to ask, that she did not ride, did not know about country life. They were effortlessly courteous and she felt a complete outsider.

'Oh, Arthur!' she thought: 'I do not belong here. We are miles apart!' and turning she met his questioning gaze.

Lunch was served by Mrs Marks, the housekeeper, and her husband, who had been maintaining for Arthur while he was away.

'This is just like old times,' she chuckled as she handed large plates of roast beef, with golden Yorkshire puddings, vegetables and thick gravy. 'It's so long since we had a family and a party here.'

'And this is right up to the old standard!' Arthur smiled back at her.

'And is this all your land?' Don asked with interest, gazing out of the window at the open park that stretched beyond the garden to the fields.

'No.' Arthur shook his head. 'In Australia, from the same sort of position I would be able to say, "yes, as far as you can see and a bit further!", but here that clump of trees marks the corner of the park and hides the road you drove up. The farmhouse over there with the land round it is mine but the land on the next hill is not.'

Imogen offered to help clear away, wondering if such things as dishwashers had yet found their way into outer Leicestershire.

'Now that would be a kindness. There's never seemed any point asking for a dishwasher when its mostly just me and my husband here. Sir Arthur lets us have the family to stay in the school holidays—but that's only for a short time. It might be different if he came back to live and we had many days like today, but I really like this the way it is.'

The large Aga cooker generously radiated warmth, sparkling dishes were ranged along the shelves of the old dressers and the scrubbed table positively invited you to start baking.

As they did the washing-up, Mrs Marks washing and Imogen drying, Imogen was amused to note that she was being very subtly interviewed.

'I'd like to have her on my staff!' she thought as she found herself answering questions about her life that were put so inoffensively that she chatted freely. At the same time she knew instinctively that nothing she said would be handed on to Arthur.

He arrived just as they were putting the last of the dishes away to ask for more coffee.

'Will you be going round the park this

afternoon?' Mrs Marks asked as she filled the pot.

'We might.' They both looked doubtfully at Imogen's shoes. 'I don't suppose Miss Gordon even has a pair of wellies!' his voice was gently teasing. 'But we could stick to the paths.'

'Now you know there's always plenty of spares if she would not mind borrowing!' Mrs Marks reproved him. 'I'll see what I can find.'

She came back to the drawing room twenty minutes later to say that she had found boots for everybody if Mr and Mrs McIntyre also wanted a stroll, and that she had turned down a bed if Mrs Enderby would prefer a nap.

'I wouldn't dare refuse!' Mrs Enderby whispered to Imogen as she went obediently upstairs.

The others found boots that fitted them well enough and Arthur called the dogs, who rushed joyously ahead of them through the trees and over the fields to the home farm, where they had to move two ponies away from a gate so that they could get through.

'They belong to the farm manager's children,' Arthur said, eyeing them critically, and Imogen was aware that he was automatically checking details as he went along in the same way that Don would as he walked over a development site. 'Do you ride at all?' The question was directed generally at all three of them. Imogen shook her head but Jenny laughed at a happy memory.

'We did a bit when we were children,' she said, 'but not like girls do today, and I doubt if you would call it riding at all!'

They came back through the stable-yards and back entrance to find Mrs Marks laying a tray for tea. She had also laid out a wonderful buffet meal for their evening guests.

'I wonder if I could ever get things so well organized,' thought Imogen, who recognized a master-hand when she met one, and found the prospect surprisingly daunting.

The guests arrived in twos and threes, all frankly curious to know if the party meant Arthur intended to stay at home now.

'I think I could be spending more time here,' he admitted, 'though there is still an awful lot of Australia to explore.'

Imogen reminded herself firmly that she was neither secretary nor hostess here, she was what she had wanted to be the evening she first met Arthur, a guest who only had to relax and enjoy herself. So why was it still not right? Why now did she wish that every time she met his glance across the room they were exchanging the coded looks she had so often observed between husbands and wives? But she still had no clue as to what he was thinking and was beginning to fear that she would reveal her own feelings and be made to feel remarkably stupid unless she was careful.

Revived by her afternoon nap Mrs Enderby was thoroughly enjoying the party, laughing and chatting gaily and looking as though she would live for a hundred years as she handed round a plateful of Mrs Marks' special canapés. She was at the other side of the room from Imogen when she suddenly collapsed with a ghastly choking sound, clutching at her throat.

Round her there seemed to be instant panic.

'Help her up . . . No! I'm sure she ought not to be moved . . . It must be stroke or a heart attack . . . a seizure . . .'

Imogen moved through the group without hesitation and taking the little old lady unceremoniously round her waist she bent her forwards and slapped her smartly between her shoulder-blades four times with the heel of her hand.

'Out. Out . . . Out!' she prayed. For a terrible moment nothing happened and she thought she had got it wrong, then the black olive that had caused the trouble fell from Mrs Enderby's lips onto the carpet, and the old lady leaned limply against her, exhausted. For a moment nobody moved, then she felt Arthur's hand on her arm.

'Well done, oh! Well done, and thank you!'

'She should lie down quietly for a bit and perhaps see a doctor.' Imogen was afraid to meet his eyes; the slight tremor in his voice had jolted her already taut emotion. 'Can you carry her?' Together they took her upstairs and tucked her into bed.

'I'll stay with her while you call the doctor,' Imogen said; without realizing it she was back into her usual managing role. 'Could we have a sponge and towel too?' She was still very worried, the old lady looked so pale and her breathing remained rapid and shallow. Arthur hurried away and she sat on the bed to hold her hand.

'Thank you, my dear! I think you saved my life . . . I haven't been so frightened in years!'

'Hush now! Don't try to talk.'

Mrs Marks appeared with the sponge Imogen had asked for, enquiring anxiously what had happened and how was Mrs Enderby now?

'She choked on an olive,' Imogen whispered, 'but I think she will be all right now.' She sponged the old lady's face gently and dried it. 'Please, you see that supper is all right and I'll stay here in case she wakes and is frightened.'

'I'll slip back in a few minutes,' Mrs Marks promised, glad to have somebody to rely on. But it was Arthur who appeared next with drinks and a plate of food on a tray.

'You must have something to eat,' he said. 'Jenny chose for you. She is being terrific downstairs. The party is rather subdued but they are having supper.' He handed her a cool glass of wine and sat by her with his own. The old lady seemed to be sound asleep. 'You were wonderful,' he went on. 'I don't know what we

51

would have done if you had not been there.'

'I am sure somebody would have thought what to do, I just happened to be nearest.'

'No, there's more to it than that. You are a really dependable person.' For a moment he looked directly into her eyes and she thought he was going to say more. He made a small movement with his hand as though to reach out to her, then suddenly had second thoughts and moved away.

'This is a lovely room,' she said. 'It doesn't feel like a spare room. It's more lived in.'

'It was my mother's, but that was a long time ago now.' He moved softly round, casting a huge shadow in the only light they had on by the bed.

'I'll get you another drink,' he said and took her glass. When he had gone Imogen started to eat her supper.

'You must be patient with him!' Mrs Enderby had opened her eyes. 'Has he told you about Nicola?'

'He told me the girl he wanted to marry decided to marry somebody else and then she was killed in a motor crash and he went to Australia,' Imogen said gently.

'That's not the whole truth. It was the sort of man Nicky chose that hurt Arthur so badly. If it had been someone he could have respected he could have faced it . . . He was so young himself, so full of ideals . . . He's a romantic . . . and he thought Nicola was

52

perfect. He put her on such a pedestal she was almost certain to fall off, poor little girl, but none of us thought she would fall so heavily. As far as he was concerned they were engaged and she was treated as the future mistress here, when suddenly she announced that she was going to marry this other man . . . He had a terrible reputation for women and they celebrated their wedding and her pregnancy in the same wild party. On the way home—or on to the next pub—he crashed the car and killed Nicola outright . . . We thought Arthur would never recover for a while . . . I don't think there's ever been anyone else.' The story seemed to have exhausted her again and her eyes closed as Arthur came back with the doctor.

It seemed that she was over the worst, but he recommended that she stayed where she was for the night if possible and he left a sedative. Mrs Marks said it was perfectly easy to look after her and Imogen, feeling suddenly tired, hoped Jenny would be ready to go home.

The party broke up quietly. Arthur's hands rested gently for a moment on her shoulders as he helped her on with her coat, as though reluctant to let her go, and she longed to lean against him, but the others were waiting. They talked very little as Don drove them swiftly home. In the darkness at the back of the car Imogen dreamed her own dreams.

# CHAPTER FOUR

The next few days took on a dream-like quality. He had her number now and each time her phone rang she suffered an unfamiliar, breathless expectancy that she had to steady before she answered.

The sun shone even when it was raining and the flowers displayed in the florists' windows had never glowed so brightly. The words of all the old romantic songs seemed true—and Imogen was scared. It was too good to be true, too wonderful to last.

'Be patient with him,' Mrs Enderby had said, but she did not want to be patient. So far he had not even really touched her but she longed for him to do so with such intensity that she feared what might happen to her either way—if the longing was denied, or if fulfilment proved disappointing. She had had no idea before that the mere anticipation could be physically painful.

In the office he was never mentioned. Such correspondence as there was about his joining the company was brief and formal. Yet his name seemed to follow her, 'Arthur, Arthur, Arthur' softly echoing her footsteps wherever she went.

Annette was slightly peevish.

'I never know where I stand with Roy,' she

said. 'Some days he's so friendly, other days he scarcely seems to know I'm here. He asked me if I liked Italian food the other day and half suggested a dinner date, but he never makes it definite.'

'I did warn you,' Imogen said dreamily, her mind on what she should wear to go to the theatre on Friday. She had already planned what to have for supper afterwards at her flat. It was just the wine that was causing her problems. She could not quite make up her mind whom to ask for advice, and suddenly she thought of the catering officer. He was always being complimented on the wines he found for their functions and on the cellar he had organized for the new hotel.

She picked up the house phone and pressed his code. They were deep in a discussion of the merits of the new Australian wines when Geoff Broadbent walked in.

'And who are you splashing out on?' he asked. 'I thought the golden boy was away!'

'Can I help you?' Imogen ignored both the question and the innuendo and wondered what he would say if she told him exactly where Arthur was in Finland at that moment—even down to the number of his hotel room. But he would be back for Friday and she could get the wine on the way home this evening.

'These are the figures Don wanted to see—the new tender.' Geoff dropped an ordinary large brown envelope on her desk. Imogen glanced at it.

'Don is not coming back to the office today,' she said. 'Do you want it sent home to him?'

'No! It can wait until tomorrow.'

'You have not put a classification on it, or sealed it,' Imogen remarked casually without intending to cause offence. But Geoff flushed angrily.

'Well I thought he was here, and I was going to hand it straight to him.' He knew perfectly well it should not have left his office unsealed and unstamped even if he had been going to hand it over personally.

'Annette will be delighted to do it for you, when she gets back from the telex room and we'll lock it in Don's safe for the night.' She put the envelope into her 'pending' tray and turned back to checking the letters.

'Do you still check all Annette's work?' Geoff asked.

'Yes! Every letter and every figure. She is one of the most careless little typists I have ever encountered—though improving,' she added generously.

'You are still dissatisfied because you wanted Cathy!' Geoff snorted as he went out.

Imogen left the post on Annette's desk and went down to Personnel for a meeting about holiday rotas. When she got back Annette had cleared the office, locking the trays in the cupboard and leaving the telephone switched through to the answering machine. Imogen

56

rang through to the main switchboard to say goodnight and hurried out. It was not until she was at home and had started on the preparations for Friday's supper that she remembered the envelope. But there was really nothing she need do about it now. It would still be in her 'pending' tray, locked in the cupboard. She had a key: Annette had a key and the only other one was with Security and Bob Shaw would not let anybody have it without her or Don's permission. It was as secure as if it was in his safe.

Arthur rang to tell her about his day and to say good night, and she went happily to sleep.

The next morning she woke with the wild idea of taking time off to go to the airport to meet him. Why not? she asked herself again and again, painfully aware of how uncertain she still was of her relationship with him. Yet he bothered to telephone her, long-distance, expensively, for no apparent reason other than that he wanted to talk to her.

'Be patient!' Would it be pushing to meet him—uninvited? She could not make up her mind and walked to work in a state of glorious indecision. Annette was already at her desk sorting through the post. She was bright-eyed and seemed to be in good spirits. Don, she said, had left a message that he would not be in until eleven.

Imogen picked up the newspapers and ran through them, marking outstanding items of interest to Don and any of their own or nearest competitors' advertising. It was a routine job and probably one that Annette should do, but she always enjoyed it herself and Annette had appeared bored by the whole idea. She could not see that she would learn anything of interest about the business she was in or the competition. Even the fashion pages were of little interest to her, she was guided only by what her crowd were wearing at the moment.

It was a very quiet day. The telephones seemed to have forgotten how to ring.

'Would you like to run down to the patisserie and get us a cream cake each to have with coffee as a Friday treat?' she suggested to Annette. The girl's eyes brightened.

'Oh! Yummy!' she said. 'What sort do you want?'

Imogen, who suddenly realized she was feeling slightly sick with excitement over the coming evening, nearly backed out.

'Just one of those small sponge splits with cream for me I think,' she said and as soon as the office door closed she grabbed the telephone and dialled the airport arrivals. At the moment, they told her, everything was going smoothly, the weather over northern Europe was clear and calm and they had no reason to expect any delays on flights in from Finland.

When Don came in she took his mail through to him and Geoff's envelope. He glanced briefly at its contents, making no comment about the lack of confidential sealing.

'Very quiet round here today,' he commented. 'If it stays like this I shall have to consider economies and cut-backs on staffing!' He grinned at her.

'Well, if you could consider a fifty per cent cut this afternoon I would enjoy having some time off!'

'All right! Weekends that start at lunch time on Friday are much better than the usual ones. Send Annette off for early lunch and then you can leave at 1.30. I have to be out for lunch myself but I will be back by two—in fact it will give me a good excuse to get away.' He started on his work and Imogen went to break the news to Annette.

Imogen loved Heathrow. She had to come out quite often to meet visitors. She checked the arrival of Arthur's flight, booked a car to take them back to town and then went up to the viewing terrace for a while to watch the constant activity all round.

By the time she returned to the arrival gate she was once again doubting if she should have come. There was still time to walk away and hurry back to her flat. For a moment she closed her eyes, and wished her heart would not race. When she opened them again it was too late to turn back. Arthur was walking towards her, laughing and talking to a gorgeous brunette with 'County' stamped all over her.

'Hello, Imogen!' he said. 'Were you sent to meet me?' She was not sure whether his smile was left over from the joke he had been sharing with the girl or if it was because she was there. 'Do you have a car waiting?'

'Yes!' Imogen smiled at them both.

'Splendid! Can we give you a lift anywhere, Ellen?'

'No thanks!' Ellen's eyes swept over Imogen without curiosity. She was completely poised and self-confident. 'I am going straight back to Leicestershire and if Daddy isn't here to meet me he will have sent someone!' Standing on tip-toe she kissed Arthur gently on his cheek and received a kiss in turn. ' 'Bye now!' and she turned with a swirl of her coat and walked gracefully away.

Arthur watched her go.

'Just a while ago,' he said, 'she was a muddy little girl on a pony. Now she's been in Finland to negotiate a time-share deal for the family's holiday chalet! How they grow up!' At that moment an elderly man stepped forward and took Ellen's case from her. 'Ah, good! She's been met,' and Arthur turned back to Imogen.

Yes, Ellen always would be met, Imogen thought. There was always a man for that type of woman, born rich and beautiful, into a

60

family where the men cossetted their womenfolk as a privilege.

'I have a car for us,' she said. 'But I was not sent. I had some free time and thought I would like to meet you. Was I wrong?'

'No! Of course not. It's very nice of you to come. I have been quite lonely these last few days amongst a lot of strangers whose only real interest in me was business. They were friendly enough but we could not really pretend to be interested in each other beyond the price tag.' He changed his case into the other hand so that he could take her arm and they walked together to the car.

On the way back he told her about his trip and the problems he had encountered, appreciating that she could follow him and understand the problems.

'Come and have a quick cup of tea with me,' he said when they reached his hotel. 'Then I will come and fetch you in time for the theatre—and no more business talk as from now!'

Imogen hurried home on the Underground and had a leisurely bath. When the bell rang she was ready to leave.

The play was good and the audience receptive. Imogen loved hearing Arthur's laughter. Whatever problems he might have he seemed to be capable of putting them right out of his mind.

'Let's go and claim our drinks,' he said as

the curtain came down for the interval. 'I'm enjoying this. It's a long time since I went to the theatre. I had forgotten how civilized it all is.'

'I thought there was a world famous opera house in Sydney,' Imogen said.

'Sydney is a long, long way from where I shack up!' he said gently and once again his eyes rested on her thoughtfully as the bell went to recall them to their seats.

Back at her flat he looked round with undisguised interest that turned to quiet approval.

'Is it all your own?' he asked. 'You do not have a flatmate?'

'No. Those days are behind me, for ever I hope!' Imogen assured him. 'This is all mine. I even decorated it myself. Not that I am very good at that—but the lighting hides the deficiencies!'

'It's the colours that matter,' he said, leaning back in her easy chair and stretching his legs in front of the fire while she got the coffee and brandy. He had seemed to enjoy his meal and recognized the wine, which had amused him.

'I thought I should try to bring a little of Australia's sunshine into your life!' she said.

'It's a very feminine room,' he went on. 'Men do not often encroach here?' It was more a statement than a question.

'I give the odd party and friends call in from

time to time, but you are right, there is not a regular male visitor! Unless you count the cat next door who calls in if I leave the kitchen window open!'

'I wonder what you would make of the shack in Australia. Perhaps you should take a holiday and come out and see it sometime. Do you have a girlfriend who would keep you company? I don't think anyone who has not experienced it first-hand can understand the heat, the dust, the loneliness. I certainly did not, though I was used to being alone. It can be disheartening.'

'I would love to see it all.' Imogen chose her words carefully. If she was ever to be with him she realized she would have to prove that she could stand a different life. But how did you prove that? There could not be a trial period. On the other hand there could be no quicker way of ending all hope than by throwing herself into his arms as she longed to do and insisting that with him she could stand anything.

The original pioneers had stood it just as they had in America, but then they could not give in so easily—no radio contact to cry for help, no planes to lift them out, scarcely a civilized city to run to. When they went they really burned their bridges or had them burnt for them.

As if he was thinking along the same lines he said, 'Of course it's easier to get out these

63

days but the experience can still be very painful for everybody.'

'Has Mrs Enderby been out to Australia?' Imogen asked suddenly.

'Indeed, yes!' Arthur laughed. 'She had my flat in Sydney for one holiday and she spent some time on the farm where we have the right things like water, cows, horses, chickens and a proper kitchen and bathroom. Then she came out to the true outback with me. She survived but we scarely did. She did her best to put things straight for us and to put us straight. She is remembered with affection and fear. Danny and Bill were with me at the time—they have never led what you would call a civilized life, although they are themselves very civilized men in that they fully understand the importance of knowing your mates and sticking together. But when water is short, drinking must come before washing, nine-to-five is unheard of and sleep may come before food.

'We had an Aborigine family who looked after things for us in a general and undefined sort of way. They disappeared like cats, but some instinct told them when she had departed and the morning after she left they were back in their shack as though they had never been away. They never told us where they had been, but neither did they deliberately undo any of the things she had done.

'And now I must be off. It's Aberdeen tomorrow for me to see an old mate in the oil trade! I would have liked to ask you to come with me but I just don't have any idea how he is living. It could be very uncivilized!'

All her hopes for the weekend dashed Imogen felt a sudden flare of irritation and wondered if he ever took a chance on anything. Was it possible, she wondered, to be too good, too careful? Was that what had driven Nicola into the arms of such a different man?

'Good night!' he said, kissing her gently. 'Thank you for the theatre and a very nice supper. See you on Monday!'

Alone again, she found herself wondering about the girl at the airport. Arthur had dismissed her as a child, but it was a fond and admiring dismissal. Was she the sort of woman he was looking for? One who had the backbone and the breeding to cope as the English aristocracy was renowned for doing . . . History was spiced with the stories of English ladies who had triumphed.

On Saturday she took herself to the zoo and looked at the kangaroos and a duck-billed platypus but they could not help with the problem because deep inside she wondered if she could cope. How efficient was she really— away from the typewriter and the telephone?

On Monday, without warning, the bottom fell out of her world. She floated into the office with only one clear idea in her golden head—that she was going to see Arthur again. But one look at Bob Shaw's face told her something was wrong.

'Sir Arthur called in very early, Miss. He left this for you.' He handed over a bulky envelope. It felt like a key. 'There's been an accident out in Australia—something to do with mining?—involving a pal of his. Anyway he's written you a note there—and he should be airborne by now—he just managed to get a flight.'

Imogen stood quite still, leaning against the security desk, trying to take it all in. Uppermost was the desolate knowledge that she was not going to see him that day after all, or for many days. And there was fear for his safety. Something told her that the 'no risk' man would take any chance to rescue a friend but in the meantime he would be suffering as only those who watch and wait can suffer from uncertainty. There would be hours on the plane with no news.

'Thanks, Bob!' she said straightening and turning to the lift.

'There's something else wrong too,' Bob said. 'I don't know what it is. But some of our leaders are in already and they're upset. There hasn't been a fire, flood or break-in but something has unsettled them! Your lad is not in yet but the others are so watch your step.'

'Oh! I wonder what it's all about?' Imogen

pressed the lift button and was carried swiftly up the floors. Bob had a keen sense for trouble but she was only concerned for Arthur.

She dropped her bag on her desk and opened the envelope before she took off her coat.

'My dear,' she read. 'I am sorry to have to dash off like this. There has been some accident in the outback and we seem to have lost all radio contact with my friends. The last messages received were rubbish.

'I have not had time to pack and anyway the stuff I have here would be no use where I am going. This is my room key. I have paid for the room for two more days, could you please go and pack for me and send the stuff to Mrs Marks in Leicestershire—and tell my Aunt and Don I will be in touch. Yours, Arthur.' He had wrapped two twenty pound notes round the key.

'So! What have we here?'

Imogen jumped, instinctively catching up the letter as Geoff Broadbent snatched the keys and the notes. She had been so absorbed reading the note she had not even heard him come into the office.

'Only forty pounds! That's just the down payment I suppose! You would hardly sell us as cheaply as that. Do you get the rest when you keep your rendezvous?' He tossed the key mockingly in the air, just out of reach. 'Come on! Hand over the letter too!'

'The letter is personal—nothing to do with you. Neither is the key, or the money. Please give them back at once!' The man was surely mad!

'You give me the letter.' Broadbent moved to come round the desk.

'Don't dare touch me!' Without really thinking what she was doing Imogen pressed the alarm button by her phone. It was part of the main security system and when the buttons had been installed it had been a rather sick office joke that all secretaries were now safe from sexual harassment. A touch of the button would summon Bob.

Except for pre-arranged tests the buttons had never been touched since their installation. Nobody was prepared for the mayhem which followed. Bells and sirens sounded everywhere and red lights flashed identifying the floor and room where the incident was taking place.

Any hope of containing the trouble in their own office was lost for ever. Imogen sank into her chair, pushing the letter deep into her pocket. She was shaking all over.

Geoff stepped away from her, his face white with fury.

'Now you have only yourself to blame for the publicity you've attracted,' he sneered as Bob and another of the security men walked in.

'Are you all right, Miss?' Bob's tough figure

suddenly took up the space between her and Broadbent. The other guard stayed by the door.

'Yes, thank you!' To her dismay Imogen found she could only whisper and she was near tears. 'Can you keep everybody out of here?'

'Yes!' Bob nodded at the man by the door. 'You had better sit down too, Sir,' he said to Broadbent as he picked up the telephone. 'Relax!' he said briefly when he was answered. 'Everything under control here but ask the nurse to come up from the first aid post—emotional upset—no wounded.'

'This is ridiculous! I shall send in a full report to . . . ' Broadbent blustered.

'That is the correct procedure, Sir,' Bob interrupted him smoothly. 'There should be three copies. One goes to the head of Security, one to your superior and one to the Company Secretary of the Consortium that owns and manages the building.'

'You will have to make a statement too, Miss, but not until after the nurse has seen you.' He spoke gently to Imogen.

'But I just do not know what it is all about,' Imogen said.

'Well, we won't bother with anything until the nurse is here.'

The offices had been built with safety in mind and it was not often the nurse had anything to do though Imogen had been told that she was prepared to cope with any crisis from a heart attack in the boardroom to a premature birth in the typing pool. She was very professional.

She examined Imogen gently but briskly, taking her pulse and feeling her face before she questioned her.

'Were you assaulted?' she asked gently.

'He threatened me—but he didn't hit me.' To her annoyance Imogen heard her voice shake again.

'She is in a slight state of shock,' the nurse spoke directly to Bob. 'I would like to take her to the sick bay.' It seemed clear that she meant 'I am taking her to the sick bay,' and Bob agreed immediately.

'Not until she has handed over that letter!' Broadbent demanded. 'That must not be destroyed. Come on—give it to me!'

Imogen shrank down in her chair, keeping her hand over the letter in her pocket.

'No!' she said. 'I have no idea why you want it. It is a personal letter—nothing to do with you!'

Bob looked at the torn envelope on her desk.

'Was that the packet I gave you this morning, Miss?' he asked.

Imogen nodded.

'Will you let me look after it? If we seal it with the other contents of that envelope until Mr McIntyre says I can give it back to you?'

Imogen hesitated. Within the building the

security men practically had police powers and she could trust Bob. He took an envelope from her desk and held it out to Broadbent who dropped the key and the money into it. Imogen handed over the letter and Bob sealed it with one of her labels and signed over the seal.

'Don't leave the first aid centre,' he said as Imogen obediently followed the nurse out of the office. It was more advice than a warning.

'Do you want anything more than a cup of tea to steady you?' Nurse asked.

'No thank you. I haven't the slightest idea what that was all about but I have a feeling that I am going to need my wits about me this morning!'

She took her tea and sat down in an easy chair. It seemed there was nothing to do but wait.

With great sensitivity the nurse busied herself quietly and did not question her.

# CHAPTER FIVE

'Could you come to the Boardroom now, Miss?' Bob spoke quietly from the door.

'Yes. Of course!' Imogen put her cup on the window sill and found to her annoyance that her hand was shaking. 'Do you have any idea what this is all about?'

71

'Enough to know that you cannot possibly have anything to worry about!' Bob replied. 'Some figures have got into the wrong hands and Mr Broadbent is looking for blood.'

Imogen caught her breath. Suddenly she saw, quite clearly, that large brown envelope, without a security seal, that was meant for Don and she had left it in her tray.

Even without the proper seal, even though she had left it in her tray, it ought to have been safe enough, she reasoned. She had failed to follow the proper office procedure to prevent something like this happening but she was not guilty of betraying the firm's confidence by handing the figures to a competitor, which was what she guessed had happened.

The consequences could still be very serious as one lost tender could easily lead to another. The integrity of the firm became questionable as well as the integrity of the people who worked there.

Don's voice came clearly as Bob opened the door for her.

'It is not for her to prove that she is innocent, but for you to prove that she is guilty, and I have no idea how this discussion was allowed to go so far without her being present.' He broke off and turned to her, his face grim.

Imogen looked round the room and felt her eyes widen. Somehow they had managed to summon the full board, including the

72

Chairman.

'Will you sit here, please!' Don indicated the chair beside his, but there was no other greeting. Imogen felt like the prisoner called to the bar.

'Good morning Miss Gordon!' The Chairman was prepared to offer some courtesy and he spoke quietly, 'Do you know what this enquiry is about?'

'No, Sir!' Imogen was now outwardly calm but inwardly she felt a deep anger stirring that she had been accused of some misdemeanour and was being summarily brought to trial without any private discussion or even the knowledge of what she was alleged to have done.

'Last Thursday Mr Broadbent gave you this envelope containing some very important figures for Mr McIntyre. At some time between Thursday and Friday when you handed the envelope to Mr McIntyre those figures were copied and the copies were sent to two of our closest competitors. One of them is almost certain now to win the contract.' He paused.

'Which contract?' Imogen asked quietly. 'We have a great many envelopes like that one and I did not look into the one I was given for Mr McIntyre.'

'It was for the Carlton Hills Complex.'

Imogen took a deep breath . . . The Carlton Hills Complex was the most prestigious plan

73

offered to them to date. Based on the assumption that the old were getting younger every day it was a new model village, complete with church and pub and also a leisure centre with swimming-pool and bowling green, tennis and badminton courts. It was hoped to attract a medley of people and make a new community. It would involve every firm in the consortium.

'Mr Broadbent admits he gave it to you unsealed but says that he asked you to do that for him. He believed you were in a position of such trust and responsibility that you would do so. As far as he knows you were the only other person to handle the envelope, the only person in a position to photocopy its contents without questions and probably the only person who knew where to market the information to its best advantage to you and to do most damage to us.'

Imogen was stunned at the meanness of the attack, but she was even more surprised at the anger she felt. 'And Mr Broadbent has made you, *all* of you, believe I did that? Why should I—and what proof have you?'

'He has reason to believe that lately you may have been tempted to raise your lifestyle rather above the level of your income. He also believes you felt slighted when you were not allowed the assistant of your choice. Then this morning you received an envelope containing some money, a key and a letter which you refused to explain.'

'And as they have nothing to do with this matter I still refuse to explain,' Imogen retorted. 'When Mr Broadbent handed me that envelope I pointed out to him that he had not sealed it correctly and, yes, he left it to me to do.

'I was in a hurry to get to a meeting and left it on my desk. Later it was locked away with other work in hand. When I gave it to Mr McIntyre neither of us had any reason to think it had been tampered with.

'But for some time it lay in my tray and somebody else could have looked at it. So it was obviously due to my carelessness that this breach of confidence occurred. I accept full responsibility and have no alternative but to give you my resignation immediately.'

She had burned her bridges and the boats now. There could be no going back on what she had said. Don was appalled.

'I really don't see that that is necessary at this point!' he exclaimed.

The Chairman was both surprised and relieved. It seemed that some of the problems raised might be quietly resolved after all, and fairly swiftly—he had a golf match to get to.

'That is the only thing you can do!' Broadbent interjected. 'Nothing can put right the damage you have done—and you still have not explained the money you received this morning.'

The Chairman sighed. Imogen realized he did not quite know what to do about it and she had no intention of making it easy for anybody—things could scarcely be more difficult for her. So she kept silent.

'Imogen! You have never been unreasonable before and I can't believe either the letter or the money can damage you in any way. Where are they now?' Don asked.

'Mr Broadbent agreed that Bob Shaw should keep them for the time being.'

'Then I suggest we get Bob in here,' Don said.

Bob arrived promptly. He looked directly at the Chairman and did not appear to notice there was anybody else in the room. His face had assumed a parade-ground mask.

'I understand Mr Broadbent and Miss Gordon had an argument this morning about an envelope containing some money, a key and a letter,' the Chairman said directly. 'To keep the peace you were given these to look after until the matter could be resolved.'

'Yes, Sir! It's Miss Gordon's property, Sir Arthur called in very early and asked me to give it to her as an emergency had recalled him to Australia. There was also a letter for Mr McIntyre which was sent to his office with the internal mail.'

'I haven't had a chance to go to my office this morning,' Don said in answer to the Chairman's unspoken question. 'I'll ring through now.' He picked up the internal phone and told Annette to find the letter and bring it up. They waited in silence. Only Bob, falling naturally into a 'stand easy' pose, was relaxed.

Annette arrived looking thoroughly scared. Imogen looked at her coldly. It was just possible that Roy was short of money again and had taken advantage of her absence from the office to look into the envelope and take copies—or even get Annette to do it so that he could get a headstart on supplying them—he would say. At least she hoped that was what had happened and not that Annette, trying to get his attention, had offered them to him. She was only guessing anyway and Don had finished reading the letter.

'Sir Arthur apologizes for not being able to give us any notice of his departure but there has been some serious accident in the outback involving one of his partners in another venture. He will be in touch as soon as possible. Meanwhile he has sent his hotel key to Miss Gordon and asked her to clear his room for him. He hopes that I do not mind him asking her to do this and that it will not interfere with her work here.'

'Will you give the envelope to Miss Gordon now, please Bob. Thank you for your help. You should be off duty by now?'

'Yes, Sir!'

'Very well—good day to you!'

Bob marched round the table and handed the envelope to Imogen. For a moment his hand touched hers and she was reassured by its warmth and firmness. She had a true friend there.

'Thank you, Bob!' It was clear that her smile and thanks were for him alone. When she turned back to the Chairman her face was set as before. 'As I am afraid there is nothing else I can do to help you, may I go now, please?'

The Chairman sighed and looked at his watch.

'You may return to the First Aid Room, Miss Gordon, while we discuss this matter a little further here.'

Feeling she was under house arrest Imogen left the room followed by Bob and Annette.

'What should I do?' Annette asked timidly.

Imogen shrugged. It crossed her mind that she was no longer in a position to give Annette any instructions at all, but out of habit she heard herself saying, 'Just go back to the office and get on with the letters or filing and take messages as usual until you are told what is happening,' and Annette scuttled away.

Bob walked on with her to the First Aid Room where Nurse greeted them with a professional smile.

'Coffee time!' she said firmly. 'You're off duty now Bob—have you time to stop for a cup?'

'I'd be very grateful for one!' Bob put his

cap and gloves on the desk and drew up a chair. He seemed quite at ease and Imogen realised that these two had a totally different view of the consortium to hers. She was inside one section of it. They were outside it all and yet belonged to all of it. They were both acute observers of people, discreet, and she wanted to talk to someone.

'Thank you for coming to the rescue, Bob. I don't know how you knew what to do but I had got myself into rather an awkward corner over Sir Arthur's letter!'

'I realize you're in a spot of bother, Miss, but I know for sure that neither you nor Sir Arthur would ever be involved in anything that was not absolutely straight. '

'I am in trouble all the same, Bob, not because I did anything wrong myself but because I was very careless and gave somebody else a wonderful opportunity that they took full advantage of.'

'And Mr Broadbent?'

'Ah! He is much higher up the ladder than I am.'

'Well, do you have anyone fighting in your corner? You belong to a union, don't you?'

'Yes, but they can't alter the facts. There has been a leak, from my office, because I was careless, and quite honestly Bob I want to go now. I just would not be happy any longer.'

'Well, don't be too hasty!' Bob warned. 'Get your contract from Personnel if you have not got a copy and make sure you are not sold short, and let your union secretary know what is going on.'

He got up to leave and Imogen smiled at him gratefully. There was nothing he could actually do, and yet knowing that he trusted her and felt for her made an enormous difference to her own outlook, because it was dawning on her that she could be in for a very testing time.

After he left, she had nothing else to do but to sit and consider her position. Her life had been so completely set. She had been on top of her job, her leisure time was organized and her holidays she spent with her mother or her sister's family. Now suddenly the ripples that had started to disturb her when she met Arthur had turned into tidal waves that threatened to sweep everything away.

Nurse was busy with a small first aid class with a cross section of junior typists, engineers and a couple of lads from the architects' department, so there was a good deal of giggling going on as they bandaged the more accessible bits and pieces of each other.

'It's a very sociable activity—we have had three weddings that we can trace to the first aid classes,' Nurse said. So against the background of their chatter Imogen began to assess her future, and realized to her dismay that she was scared!

It was one thing to work in a well-regulated

rut surrounded by every piece of modern technology in a job into which she had grown, but she suddenly realized it was the only job she had ever had! Nobody had ever questioned her qualifications or her ability, she had never applied for anything else or had an interview, never had to compete on the open market.

But, most worrying of all, who would Arthur hear from first, and what would he hear? Their love was still too new, too tender to take a shock like this. He had been let down once already and she felt that if he thought she had done anything dishonest he just would not bother to get in touch even when he could.

'I might have known,' she sighed to herself. 'It was too wonderful to last. In spite of all that Maude says that there is romance there for everyone who keeps their hearts open there is no guarantee that it will end in happily ever after.'

'Are you all right?' Nurse was bending over her anxiously. 'You've gone very pale.'

'I think it's called shock!' Imogen smiled ruefully. 'I have just realized I've lost a job and a whole way of life in one moment's carelessness!'

'Oh! It can't be that bad!' Nurse soothed her. 'I have heard nothing but good things about you and your boss. I am sure you can work something out.'

The telephone rang, summoning Imogen back to the boardroom. She returned to her seat next to Don and looked at the Chairman.

'Miss Gordon, I hope you will understand this is very difficult for all of us. We shall all be very sorry to see you go, particularly in these circumstances.'

Imogen looked across at Broadbent and held his gaze for a long moment. She thought he looked delighted.

'We feel we have no alternative but to accept your resignation and will check your contract to decide the terms under which we should do so. It is never a happy situation to work under the stress of leaving. We would suggest that you return to your office now with Mr McIntyre and we will send somebody up as soon as possible to take over from you. Do you think you could hand over to them this afternoon?'

'Of course. Everything is in order, and very straightforward.' Imogen hardly recognized her own voice. 'This must be what a candle feels like when it's blown out,' she thought.

'Very well! Good bye, Miss Gordon!' The Chairman stood up and turned to go back to his office. Imogen followed Don to the lift in silence. He waited until they were safely back in their own domain before he exploded.

'Imogen! What on earth possessed you to behave like that ?'

It was tempting to tell the truth, to say, because I am in love I've grown absent-minded. I forgot to seal that wretched envelope. I made it easy for someone to tamper with it.

'It was serious, yes! But you hadn't done anything wrong—Broadbent should have sealed it himself before he gave it to you. We could have ridden this thing out!'

'No, Don. It would never have been the same. Everybody believed I had sold those figures and nobody thought that I might have a perfectly honourable life of my own outside the office.'

'This is diabolical! I never thought you had sold them! Though I could not understand how you could have been so careless—it's totally unlike you. But it's not a resigning matter.'

'I think it is. I was asked to seal it. I didn't. So there was a leak and it was my fault—and anyway, Don,' she softened her voice deliberately, 'don't you think that perhaps it is time I moved on? I have been so happy working for you—and it's ten years now! But it's changed you know.

'When we started it was just you and me against the world and Jenny doing the books for you. You needed me then. But now any well-trained secretary could do the job. You don't really know the people you build for any longer. You are a tremendous success but you are a property developer now—not a small time builder.'

'Damn it all, Imogen! You are my right hand and part of my brain. You are

83

responsible for a great part of that success! Who will I get now?'

'Judging by the way my recommendation was ignored when the question was raised a little while ago I don't think anybody will take any notice of my advice now,' Imogen said bitterly.

But it was Cathy who appeared soon afterwards to take over temporarily—an uneasy, unhappy Cathy who clearly saw herself as an usurper. They worked quietly through the diary and the files bringing her up to date. Imogen found most of her emotional energy was used reassuring her that she was up to the job and not taking advantage of her misfortune.

'Don likes you, Cathy! and I think you will find this is made a permanent appointment very soon.'

Annette was unusually subdued and the older girls made little reference to her.

The Personnel Officer appeared soon after lunch and, as often in difficult situations, Imogen was thankful for formality. Her dismissal went as smoothly and unemotionally as any minor business transaction. A month's severance pay to be paid into her bank at the end of the following month; an account of the company shares she had been given and the time they were to be left with the company; instructions as to how to transfer her pension insurance to another firm or to a private plan;

her personal documents—everything she could need to know and might not have thought to ask about was neatly packaged for her to take away.

'Will you phone me sometime—let me know you are all right?' Cathy's voice shook a little.

'Of course! I would like to meet you outside the office. You'll do a great job here!'

The final moment had come. Imogen put on her coat and went and tapped on Don's door. She had prepared a little speech but suddenly there was nothing to say and the tension between them was unbearable.

'Goodbye, Don!'

'Goodbye, Imogen! Refer any future employer direct to me, either at home or on my private line here. There is no need to go through the usual channels.' He turned to look out of the window and did not watch her go.

The lift took her alone, swiftly and silently, down to the ground floor. She seemed to have become invisible for all the notice anyone took of her as she crossed the foyer to the great revolving door. She pushed her way out into the street at the unfamiliar time of 3.30, all the personal belongings from her desk hastily packed into a plastic bag.

She walked slowly along the street, absent-mindedly dodging other pedestrians. If she had ever had any plans for an unexpected afternoon off she could not now remember what they were. Suddenly there was no reason for her to be anywhere.

She remembered how, when she was a little girl, her cat had been hit by a car or a motorcycle, he had crept in, badly injured, after being missing for twenty four hours and she had wept while she waited for the vet to see him. The vet had been concerned for her.

'You are lucky he came home,' he said. 'Often when they are hurt they just creep away and don't seem to make any effort to get back to where they will be cared for. I can't make any promises but I think you can take this as a good sign that we may be able to make him better. You'll have to leave him with me for a day or two and we'll see how he goes.'

Now, like an injured animal, she did not want to go back to her flat. She could ring her mother, who would be horrified that she had lost her job. She could ring her sister, who would also be horrified that she had lost her job but would add that there was plenty for her to do if she came to stay with them for a bit. Imogen did not want to talk to either of them.

She wandered into a coffee bar and sat for some time until she realized it was self-service. Hunting through her handbag for her purse she found Arthur's key. She might as well go and clear his room. It would be something to do.

She walked to the hotel.

'That's all right, Miss. We've been expecting you,' the porter said. 'Just ring down when you have finished packing and I'll carry the bags down for you and get a cab.'

She unlocked the door feeling that she was intruding on Arthur's private space, wondering if she would feel his presence, wishing that she could. But all his most intimate possessions had gone with him. Those that were left did nothing to subdue the impersonality of the hotel bedroom.

She found two cases and put them open on the floor by the dressing-table, then she went systematically through the drawers and cupboards and laid everything on the bed to fold and pack.

Never had she felt so alone or so lonely. She had to keep stopping to blow her nose and the tears were very near the surface. Finally she found the laundry bag in the bathroom, containing two shirts, some socks and pants. She could send them to Mrs Marks, who would be delighted to see to them. But she suddenly wanted to do them herself.

Bundling the last things into the cases she snapped the lids shut and pulled the leather straps tight over the locks. She could see to them this evening and then tomorrow she could decide the best way to send the whole lot to Leicestershire.

# CHAPTER SIX

'Keep busy!' had always been her mother's instruction when things went wrong. 'Don't sit and brood!' It had been so long since things had gone wrong—really wrong—that Imogen thought she had forgotten how to cope. She felt as though she had been capsized into water which was deeper and colder than she thought it was.

Arthur's few things would not be a washing-machine load by themselves. She went through her own drawers and cupboards at furious speed, cramming things into the laundry and dry cleaning bags and filling plastic carriers with things she thought she was sick of for the local charity shop.

There would have to be a new beginning and subconsciously, as she checked the clothes for spots or loose buttons, she was planning to leave. How had she ever collected so much, she wondered. By the time it was in three piles—for keeping, on the bed; for jumble, by the door; for the laundrette, by the window—it was too late for the dry-cleaner to take anything anyway, but the laundrette would still be open.

Picking up a book to while away the time she went down to the laundrette and found herself mindlessly watching the clothes twirling together, the book unopened on her lap. America . . . in the past she had had various offers of work over there, and she had always kept the contacts—but it would take time and she wanted immediate release. She would have to decide what to do now. She thought she made decisions easily, every day, but now she could not find a starting point.

'If that's your machine—it's stopped, dearie!' For a moment Imogen looked blankly at the speaker, a tiny little old woman, bent and twisted with arthritis, wrapped in an old tweed coat with a brown beret crammed on her head. 'You all right?' the interrogative black eyes were surprisingly bright.

'Yes, yes . . . thank you!'

'You looked a bit lost to me.' The old lady stood beside her contemplating the washing as Imogen took it out of the machine, Arthur's shirts entangled with her nighties. 'Having problems with him?' The blatant curiosity made Imogen smile.

'Not the way you're probably thinking,' she replied good naturedly. 'I never really had him, and now I rather think I've lost him along with my job.'

'Broke?'

'No!'

'Then I'd call that 'freedom'. Strapping young lass like you these days, with your looks . . . reckon I'd have gone places!'

'And what did you do?' Imogen asked gently

looking at the heavy, old fashioned wedding ring on the misshapen hand, and wondering why, just because she was tall, she was always expected to be able to cope even when her heart was breaking!

'I was a cook . . . married a good man. We had enough. We used to go dancing and to the pictures.' Her voice was softer almost dreamy for a moment. 'We had good times . . . But it's all different now with money, cars, holidays . . . you can go places like we never could!' She spoke with energy but without rancour. 'I'd just take off if I could . . . There! There's my little lot done.' They went on to the dryers together.

'And now . . . do you have a family?' Imogen wondered if it was safe to ask.

'Just a daughter and her husband took her off to Scotland. We see each other a couple of times a year.' And she watched silently as the sheets fell through the hot air of the dryer. Imogen helped her fold them before she gathered her own lot together.

'Would you like to live with her?'

'Not now, dearie. I'm easier with folk my own age. But you're young. You've a lifetime ahead of you!'

Home again, she nearly left the ironing till the morning, but the habit of finishing all the jobs possible in the evening, to leave the next day clear was too strong. She switched on the television, got out the board, and slowly, carefully began to iron Arthur's shirts.

It took longer than she expected. Once, she remembered, she had heard two older women discussing the domestic problems of one of their children.

'She doesn't really care any longer,' one of them opined. 'You just look at his shirts—they're scarcely washed—let alone ironed! My mother always used to say that the first thing a wife resents doing for her husband when she's falling out of love with him is his laundry—and it's as true today as it was then!'

At the moment Imogen could see no hope of ever doing Arthur's laundry again, but at least this lot would stand up to Mrs Marks' scrutiny. The collars were perfect and she eased the point of the iron neatly into the pleats and gathers at the cuffs.

In a surge of fantasy she slipped out of her dressing-gown and put the last shirt on herself before she folded it. The freshly laundered material was cool and soft against her skin and her fingers trembled as she fastened the lower buttons to her own cleavage. It was too big for her but, roused, her nipples thrust against the fine cotton, two dark, peaked roundels and she felt suddenly exposed as though he were lying on the bed watching her.

Hastily, as though afraid of being caught in some clandestine act, she dropped the shirt to the floor, put on her dressing-gown again and returned to the legitimate task of re-packing the cases. It was long after midnight before she was satisfied that everything was correctly stowed away. She fastened and locked the catches and wrote fresh labels, feeling that she was banishing him forever, packing him out of her life.

It was only when she came to put away her own things that she found the white lawn handkerchief, folded into a precise square. Well, she could put it into the envelope with the keys and the little note she would have to write to Mrs Marks. For a moment she held it against her cheek, then, very deliberately she opened her handbag, pushed it into an inner pocket and closed the zipper. He would never miss it.

She never needed to set the alarm and could not at first think what bell it was that broke her uneasy, early-morning dream.

Arthur! Wide awake, she flung the downie off the bed and ran through to the sitting room.

'Hello! Hello!' Her voice broke with anxiety, but it was Jenny's soft voice that came gently down the line.

'Imogen! Are you all right? I would have rung you last night but I was out of town all day and Don did not tell me what had happened until very late. My dear, he is so upset! Do you have to go off like this—is it really a resigning matter?'

'I am sure Don gave you a very fair and

accurate account of what happened,' Imogen made herself speak slowly. 'You must see there was nothing else I could do!'

'I think you are taking far too much of the blame!'

'Maybe . . . but I do not feel I would ever be trusted again, and I can't work like that.' Imogen sighed.

'Well, I always realized you would leave us one day, but I never thought it would be like this. Have you enough money to be going on with . . . What are you going to do?'

'I hardly know yet . . . what I'm going to do I mean . . . but yes, I do have enough saved up to see me through, thank you!'

'Well, I am going to send you a little present anyway, my dear, and you must promise me you will let me know how you are and where you are. I would be so very unhappy if we lost touch.'

Imogen hesitated. Her main idea at that precise moment was to put as much space as possible between herself and her life as it had been; but Jenny was dear to her for herself, not for what she could do as the boss's wife.

'Jenny! I'm terribly mixed up at the moment. It was all so sudden.' She tried desperately to control the tears in her voice. 'I will write to you. Thank you for ringing. Good-bye now.' She could not go on talking but put the phone down gently before she started to cry.

Aunt Maude always said that there was nothing like a good cry when things went wrong, but it was a feminine reaction that Imogen had always felt she had to deny herself. She was surprised to discover how very therapeutic it was.

Ten minutes later, with the hot water in the shower streaming through her hair, she felt full of determination. She dressed with as great care as though she was going to the office on board-meeting day, but as there was no hurry, she indulged in extra toast for breakfast. Then she called a taxi, loaded it with Arthur's cases and her own packages and set off on the first stage of clearing the flat.

That was the easy bit, she realized. In fact it seemed very difficult just to leave home even though she only had herself to consider. Day after day she read of, or heard of, people who simply walked out, but how did they do it, she wondered? What happened to their possessions, contracts, agreements?

She paid off the taxi and started on foot in the general direction of home, trying to savour this unexpected freedom—nothing special to do at eleven o'clock on a work-a-day morning. In the office the coffee cups would be cleared away by now, and, bolstered by routine, even the late starters would be putting on a show of industry.

Sale notices in a boutique drew her across the street to a cheerful little shop where a young lady in a brightly coloured trouser suit, her tousled hair heaped loosely on top of her head, was eager to serve her. Imogen, who would have preferred to browse, felt obliged to make conversation. The 'Clara' label on the clothes was the same design as the name over the shop front.

'Is this your own business?' she asked, pausing on her way down the dress rail.

'Yes! I had to scrub floors to get it!'

'Scrub floors?'

'To begin with I worked nights as a cleaner, designed and made clothes in the day and slept all Sunday—my Mum insisted on that! Then, when it looked as though I could make a go of it the family scraped a bit together for me and I got the end of the lease here cheaply. Now I still do all the designing but I have friends who do sewing for me.'

'They're nice things—nicely finished,' Imogen said. Really it would be stupid to buy anything just now; she ought to be saving money and anyway she had no idea what sort of clothes she would need in the future. She picked a shirt off another rail and held it up against her face, and was surprised how the mix of blues and greens in the fabric deepened the colour of her eyes.

'It suits you—the colour I mean,' Clara said.

'My life is changing so fast at the moment I don't really know what I do want . . . I don't think I really even know who I am . . .' To her dismay Imogen heard her voice falter, but Clara was unembarrassed, instantly concerned.

'You look as though you manage your life very well.'

'I had a good job,' Imogen responded, 'and I thought I was good at it!'

'But you are much more than your job!' Clara sounded shocked. 'You are more than the sum of your job, your family and your friends. Even if they are all swept away you are still you. I have to change too—the lease is up here so I am off to Canada to join forces with a girlfriend.'

'I'm beginning to think I've led a very sheltered life!' Imogen said gravely—the girl could not be a day over twenty, she thought and I feel a generation away from her. 'I'll take the shirt,' she said,' and when I wear it I shall think of you starting all over again in Canada!'

'You'll be all right, you'll see!' Clara said encouragingly. 'And if you ever come to Saskatoon you look out for me!'

Imogen wished her luck, took her parcel and resumed her walk home, wondering if Arthur had tried to ring her at the office and if he had what reply Cathy had given him. Perhaps she should have left some message, but she just did not know what to say. But it was unlikely that he had even tried to contact her. His messages had made it quite clear that the only thing that concerned him at the moment was the safety of his partner.

Everything else would have to wait until he knew, one way or the other, what had happened to him.

If only she had some way of knowing if Arthur himself was safe. Where was he? Still in Sydney trying to find out if there was any news or already setting out to find his friend? She had absolutely no idea how such an operation was mounted—only his laughing assurance in the pub on their first date that he never set off into the desert without knowing exactly where the water was to be found! He had made it quite clear that there was no margin for error, no tolerance for carelessness, no place for people like herself who made stupid mistakes.

She might just as well make up her mind that she would never see him again, that there was no point in remembering the warm touch of his hand on hers, his smile when he thanked you, or the way he considered some idea you had put forward that was new to him.

When he came back, if he came back, and heard why she had had to leave he would never bother to try to find her.

Well, St Cuthman had pushed his poor old mother eastwards in the barrow; Arthur had set off for Australia; the old lady in the laundrette was obviously surprised that she could not see her good fortune; and Clara was setting off for Canada.

'Whether 'tis nobler in the mind to suffer

the slings and arrows of outrageous fortune; or to take arms against a sea of troubles and by opposing end them?' From *Hamlet* she thought, and if she had got it right maybe her English teacher would be proud of her. But Hamlet, she rather thought, had come to a sticky end through thinking too much but never actually doing anything until it was too late.

Gradually her resolve to leave was firming and as she attacked the flat, cleaning each room as it had never been cleaned before, she mulled over where to go. Funny! When she day-dreamed in the past or watched television travelogues there were thousands of places to go to. Now none of them seemed the least bit attractive—except Australia and that was out of bounds.

Early in the evening she went down to the basement flat and rang the bell on the inner door, which told her landlady it was one of the tenants calling.

'Why! Miss Gordon! Are you not well? I thought I saw you come in early today and you didn't go out again. I said to myself I said, Miss Gordon's home early and it's not like her to miss work. I hope she's not been taken bad, I said.' In the half-light of the basement passage she peered at Imogen with curiosity rather than concern.

There was no love lost between Miss Crawford and any of her tenants. They were all convinced she went through their mail boxes if she got the opportunity and she had an uncanny knowledge of their comings and goings. Imogen had long ago learned to parry her insistent queries, so now she smiled brightly and said, 'I'm fine, thank you Miss Crawford, but I have to be away for some time, certainly into the next rent period, so I have come down now to pay you in advance.' She handed over her cheque and rent book. Miss Crawford relaxed at the sight of the money, as Imogen knew she would.

'Come along in,' she said, 'while I fill in the books.' Imogen followed her into the cluttered sitting-room but she did not sit down. 'And where might you be going?' Miss Crawford asked.

'Oh we have a lot on!' Imogen replied cheerfully. 'I might even get to America for a while. I will let you know if anything happens to delay my return. Now, I do not want the office bothered with any of my personal affairs so I have written my Aunt Maude's name and address here,' she handed over another piece of paper. 'You remember my Aunt, she has called here several times—Mrs Chisholme ? I shall be in touch with her and I would be grateful if you would forward any odd mail that comes for me to her.'

'That is exciting for you! Promotion is it?' Miss Crawford could not contain her curiosity.

'It's different anyway!' Imogen said and

made for the door before she could be trapped into any further discussion. Miss Crawford had been very impressed by Aunt Maude and was quite content to go along with anything she knew about. Arthur's visit caused no comment—unlike the pretty little hussy on the second floor, Imogen smiled wryly to herself, Miss Gordon did not have any interesting gentlemen friends!

Before she could have second thoughts she dialled Aunt Maude and was fortunate to catch her between the bath and her dressing-table as she changed for dinner.

'Where are you going?' she asked.

'To the Admiral's, alas!'

'What do you mean—alas!—You enjoy meeting all those gallant naval types!'

'Yes, dear! But that frightfully clever sister of his is going to be there too—the one who is so gimlet-sharp at bridge and backgammon.'

'Well that shouldn't worry you! You play a very sharp game of bridge yourself.'

'Umph! Well, she implies that I play on my looks and the men are lenient with me!'

'And don't you . . . and aren't they?' Imogen was highly amused. 'I suppose you are wearing blue?'

'No, dear!—Beige!'

'Now I know you are having me on! You are as likely to wear beige as Barbara Cartland is!'

Maude giggled at her end of the line.

'Actually darling, it's creamy with a deep

100

purple shawl collar which sort of twists down to become a hip line sash . . . It's very dramatic and I hope I am not asked how much it cost! It's certainly a change . . . But tell me now . . . How are you and why did you ring?'

'Well, I'm making a few changes.' She tried to sound confident and light-hearted, but it did not work with Maude, who knew her far too well.

'I do see the difficulty of going on working there, dear,' she said. 'But what about this lovely Australian man Jenny was telling me about when I bumped into her in Harrods the other day? Did she tell you we had met? . . . No? I don't suppose she has had time with all the fracas . . . Oh! Imogen, darling, I really had great hopes for you there!'

'So did I! . . . Oh Maude it's wonderful having someone I can be completely honest with . . . I really thought I had found someone special at last . . . I know I had—but he is really very special and I am sure he just won't be interested in me at all, if he ever comes back and finds out how I let everybody down . . . He just doesn't have room for anybody like that.' And she burst into tears.

'Oh, Moggy!' Maude reverted to her childhood pet-name for her. 'I am sure he is not as uncompromising as that! It's one thing to have high standards but quite another to be unable to forgive an error! Jenny thought he was a very straight, gentle man, not an ogre!'

'The sort of life he leads he can't afford to take chances on people letting him down.' Imogen blew her nose and wiped her eyes with what was already a very damp handkerchief. 'We were really only just getting to know each other—we had only been out a couple of times when he had to dash back to Australia. I really don't have any reason to think he was so interested in me that he will worry if I am not there when he gets back.'

'Well, why don't you just pack your things and come and stay quietly with us until he gets back—then we'll see.'

'Oh, Maude, you are wonderful—but I can't do that! I'm sorry but I just could not take the humiliation of his ignoring me. No, I have got to get right away and prove I can manage by myself. Now, you remember meeting my weird landlady . . . well I have asked her to forward my mail to you. Please would you just keep it for me?'

'But where are you going?'

'To York—but please don't tell anyone. Just say I have got a temporary job out of town and I am looking round.'

'But have you?' Maude sounded worried.

'No. But I think I know someone up there who can help me. Now I must not make you late!' And suddenly she found she had made up her mind what to do.

As soon as they had rung off she slid from the bed, dragged out her largest suitcase and packed carefully and methodically. In the morning she got up early, finished the tidying and packing and she was ready to go.

It was such a tiny flat but she had made it hers, a haven, a home to come back to each day. She went round it once more, stroking the doors and walls, touching the cushions and pictures. Then she drew the curtains half across the windows and went to find a taxi.

One more journey up the stairs to collect her cases and her roots would be torn up. With her cases on the landing she paused for one final look across the room. She would leave Arthur sitting in her chair as he had been the night he came to dinner.

'Goodbye!' she whispered as she closed and locked the door. She dropped the keys into the pocket of her handbag with the handkerchief. 'Kings Cross, please!' she said to the cab driver and she did not look back.

## CHAPTER SEVEN

The Inter City 125 deposited her in York two hours later with very little recollection of the journey. If her body could have followed her mind she would have arrived in Australia. A young man whose leather jacket, unkempt hair and tattoos were belied by his gentle Scots accent and smile helped her out of the train and lifted down her heavy case.

'You're making a long stay,' he said, 'enjoy it!' and he waved as he jumped back on board leaving Imogen alone on the platform. Perhaps she should have gone right on up to Aberdeen too, she thought, as she lifted the case and set off over the foot-bridge to the exit. At least it was an open station so she did not have to fumble for a ticket at the barrier. There were plenty of taxis too, but she still had not made up her mind where to go.

For a full two minutes she stood, undecided, in the main hallway looking across the wide road to the grass banking topped by the city wall. In the spring, she had been told, they were covered with daffodils. Now they were a featureless green and returned her look with indifference.

There was no point in humping her case round with her. She checked it into the left luggage office, bought a street guide, and set off on foot through the walls into the city. The Minster, rising among the other buildings on the far side of the river, seemed the obvious place to start.

Crossing Lendal Bridge with its brightly painted crests she paused to look up the wide river. There were some small boats moored below the walls with attendant shelducks circling in the grey water. Two rowing fours shot under the bridge immediately beneath her and raced away upstream to the railway bridge. Downstream buildings came closer to the water, and she could see more people and traffic hurrying over a stone bridge, but it was too cold to linger. If she could get a job, or even if she could not for a day or two, there would be plenty of time to explore.

She went on towards the Minster which, rising straight from the pavement, seems to be so much part of the fabric of the city. But before she reached it she found a pleasant and uncrowded café and decided to have some lunch and study her guide.

She had been telling Maude the truth when she said she had a contact in York. She had never met Gloria Holden but they had talked quite a lot on the telephone. Gloria ran an employment agency and seemed to have good contacts. She had supplied them with temporary staff at short notice when they were planning and building the northern complex and she had head-hunted for several firms. If there was anything going for Imogen she ought to be able to find it.

Imogen ordered a salad and baked potato lunch with a glass of wine and studied her guide. Petergate? Ah! There it was—very close. She was surprised in fact how small York was—the Minster, the theatres, museums almost within touching distance of each other. She ate her lunch slowly—rather wishing now that she had rung Gloria earlier. Mentally she went over what she could say to explain her

105

predicament without sounding unemployable, and feeling better for something to eat she paid her bill and crossed the road briskly to the phone box.

Miss Holden was in and, yes, she remembered her and could see her at three o'clock. If she was curious she gave no indication of it. Imogen went on towards the Minster trying to fit a face to the calm, efficient voice on the phone.

The Minster, grand though it was, failed to hold her as Ripon had. Was it just that Arthur was not there to bring everything to life? She spent a little time in front of the astronomical clock, dedicated to the Royal Air Force, and crossed the nave to look up at the recently restored rose window. Even without sunlight the colours glowed and the workmanship that had gone into such a faithful restoration of an historic building was something she could appreciate.

As she looked at the pictures of the fire that had devastated the south transept she could imagine the feelings of the people who loved and worked in the place as they stood among the water-sodden ruins the next morning. Only the day before, they had seemed to be putting all their available energy into keeping the vast building in a good state of repair, yet always they were falling behind. Then the lightning struck, presenting them with a seemingly impossible task—but they had won!

Perhaps the two situations really could not be compared but surely the havoc her carelessness had created was not as serious as this had been, and Don had twice as much determination as anybody else. While Arthur, who had already decided to cut women out of his life, would regard the whole sorry episode as yet another example of female fallibility and help to pick up the pieces without her.

So once again he was at the centre of her thoughts and she was bewildered by the clarity with which she could sense him. Every detail was etched on her mind. Surely if she turned now she would find she was looking just slightly up into his deep brown eyes and the light would catch the few silver hairs that had already appeared at his temples and in his beard, and he would put out his strong, sun-tanned hand to guide her to the next part of the Minster. She made herself move forward and there was no footfall behind her.

She found a tiny chapel set aside for private prayer and sat for a while, thinking about him, asking only for his safety. Then she hurried out to her appointment. She only had a slightly battered life to heal and the bruises were all of her own making.

Gloria Holden was rather younger than she expected but otherwise very like her voice on the telephone, positive, quiet and friendly enough to make an interview easy.

'So! It's nice to meet you at last, and what

brings you to York?'

Imogen met her eyes and realized that here was a woman who could detect a lie with absolute precision.

'I need a job,' she said with a smile. 'Any job, temporarily, if I can't find the right one straight away—I have some quite good contacts in America I think—but you can never tell how good a contact is until you have tested it, can you? If you will take me on you probably have better ones.'

'And are you testing me?' Gloria's laugh was full of merriment.

'Oh! I'm sorry. That must be how it sounded but it wasn't what I meant!'

'It sounded very honest! I think you are in an unexpected situation and one that you are unused to handling—and I am surprised because I got the impression you were immovable.'

Imogen watched the pigeons on the next roof for a moment before she replied.

'I had never thought about moving,' she admitted, 'but then something unexpected happened that made me re-assess . . . everything—and it seemed the wisest course.'

'But why here? Most girls seem to want to go south!'

'I wanted to go somewhere quite different and . . . yes . . . I suppose that consciously or subconsciously I remembered you and thought York would be a good place to start.'

'Well I can tell you straight away that at present I do not have anything to offer you that is remotely like the job you have left and I really cannot send you to any of the temporary jobs I have at present—you're just too good for them!'

'I could keep a low profile,' Imogen suggested.

'Not low enough I'm afraid, but,' Gloria hesitated, tapping her teeth with a perfectly manicured fingernail, 'are you really ready to try anything—temporary?'

'That sounds like an awful warning, but the answer is still 'yes' I am.'

Gloria pressed her intercom button.

'Jessie,' she said when her receptionist answered, 'have you replied to Mr Torrance yet?'

'No, Miss Holden, there really has not been time and as you flagged it low priority I put it to the bottom of the pile. I think I shall have it ready for tomorrow morning's post—sorry!'

'That's all right. Would you bring it in here please and make us a cup of tea—thank you. This is not the sort of job I usually take on,' Gloria explained to Imogen, 'but I have found staff for Mr Torrance and his firm—they are accountants in Scarborough by the way— Shawl, Shawl and Harrison, well enough known up here with branches in York and Leeds and even Sheffield. Now he is in a bit of a jam—his wife, who is a veterinary surgeon—

went out to Australia on a working holiday, leaving Mr Torrance and three children in the care of her mother. All went well for a few weeks, but then her mother fell in the farmyard—they live on a remote farm some way outside Scarborough by the way—and she broke her pelvis and injured her spine. Meanwhile Mrs Torrance in Australia has been involved in a motor accident and will be in hospital for at least another four weeks.

'He thought he could manage but now says the children need more care as he is often home late, so he is looking for temporary domestic help. How do you feel about that?'

'Terrified!' Imogen replied. 'I mean how old are the children . . . and doesn't he want somebody with a proven record of cooking and cleaning?'

'No! In fact his letter is rather negative. He says,' Gloria flipped through the file Jessica had brought in, ' "I am looking for someone who is not under twenty-five and not over forty, who is neither widowed nor divorced, and is not looking for a husband. She should also not have any mental or physical frailty that means we end up looking after her! If she cannot manage without the bright lights for a month she will not do! Through your many contacts can you find me someone? P.S. I don't like nurses!" '

'Frankly, I did not even have time to begin

to look—but, it could be a blueprint for you! You've never been a nurse, have you? . . . The children are . . . ten, twelve and fifteen—two girls and a boy, but he does not say which age belongs to which—at least they are not helpless.'

Imogen had recovered her breath.

'For a man desperate for help he does not expect much, does he?' she suggested. She had a feeling there was something else Gloria knew and was not telling. 'I can cook,' she went on '—at least I produce meals for myself and my friends and when I go home or to my sister's I cook for the family. I keep my own flat clean and at my mother's house I push a hoover round but I would never claim that I can necessarily do any of those things to a professional standard.'

'You are amazingly honest!' Gloria replied. 'Most people are convinced that they can cope with a house with one hand tied behind them. Do you want to give this man a try?—After all it's only for a month . . . But he will want references—he is letting you into his home, to be with his children.'

'Well Mr McIntyre said I was to ask anyone to refer to him direct, so did the Personnel officer. I think you would find them both in the office this afternoon if you wanted to use the phone and they would follow it up with a letter, but I don't know anbody off hand who would vouch for my suitability looking after children—except for a very limited time with my baby niece, I just haven't any experience.'

'You have your tea,' Gloria said, 'and help yourself to a biscuit while I get busy on the phone and we'll see what happens!'

She was gone for some time. Imogen finished her tea and relaxed in her chair, her eyes closing. She was desperately tired, but maybe things were moving. The urgent ring of the Fax machine broke through her drowsiness just before Gloria came back and she pulled herself upright again in her chair.

'Everything seems fine,' Gloria said. 'Your references are great—they faxed them through to me straight away, and Mr Torrance asks if you can start today?'

'Why not, if he wants me to?' It meant abandoning a half-formed plan to look round York, but she might well not have enjoyed being alone and a hotel would have cost quite a bit.

'Right! Well then, here's what you will have to do. He's at a meeting till rather late this evening, so he would like you to go on to Scarborough by train and go to the Victoria Hotel. Get yourself a decent meal, which he will pay for when he picks you up—he's well known there and he will tell them to expect you. He will come and pick you up as soon as he can and drive you out to the farm. Can you cope with that?'

'Er . . . yes. I think I shall have to get a pair

of jeans or something and different shoes, and do I get any sort of contract with this type of job?'

'Well if you like to go shopping I will write up an agreement for you—I said you wanted £100 a week and your keep—that way it looks sufficiently respectable for him to put it on the firm's books as secretarial help and they can cope with your tax etc. as well. He was a little stunned at first but I pointed out that your hours would be long and your responsibilities heavy. I hope that's all right—I did not think I would get any more out of him and you will be living free!'

'I am sure you are right—I had not even thought what to ask, but I would like to make it a four week agreement with the option to review the situation when we know how his wife is.'

She returned to the office an hour later having had quite a good time buying jeans, cords and trainers and a new sweater, also, in what turned out to be an inspired moment, a pair of household gloves. Gloria had an agreement ready for her to sign and a faxed copy already signed by Bernard Torrance.

Imogen studied the signature with interest. It was large and clear but rather flamboyant, she thought, and the main down and cross strokes looked aggressive. It would be interesting to know about graphology but as she knew nothing it was silly to speculate.

'I am not really used to being picked up in hotels by strangers,' she said to Gloria. 'What sort of man am I expecting—do you know him by sight?'

'Oh!—he's very presentable!' Gloria smiled. 'The tall, dark handsome type—but a bit creased now—has a good, low voice and is always very well dressed. I am sure he will not make you feel you are being "picked up"!'

'Thanks! And thank you for all your help. I'll let you know how I get on, if I may.'

'Yes, do! And if it's too ghastly, leave!'

Imogen made her way back to the station and collected her cases. She hoped he would not be very late. Her own comfortable flat suddenly seemed very desirable and very far away, but the little local train to Scarborough was standing at the platform and she heaved her suitcase on board for the last leg of the journey.

The evening was drawing in and a cold east wind was bringing a mist in from the North Sea. The train rattled along carrying local commuters who had no interest beyond getting home and forgetting another day. She could see little of the country they were going through, but was mildly amused to work out that although it only took two hours to travel from London to York it still took nearly an hour to go from York to Scarborough; and by the time they reached it the mist had given way to pouring rain.

Imogen stood just inside the station and pondered her next move. The hotel was on the other side of the rainswept road—too far to carry her cases with any ease or comfort, but not nearly far enough to warrant a taxi. But if she left them at the station there would be difficulties picking them up later.

'May I borrow a trolley to take my cases over the road?' she asked the elderly porter hopefully.

'The lad here's just going off, love! He'll carry them for you.'

The lad proved to be a young man about six and a half foot tall with hands like Yorkshire hams. He picked up Imogen's cases as though they were a couple of feather pillows and strode across the road keeping to windward of her to shield her from the rain.

She wondered briefly at this unusual protectiveness for her person, but then she caught sight of her pale, strained face in the foyer mirror. Strands of blond hair had escaped their restraining side-combs and her eye make-up was smudged. Also she discovered she had reached that low ebb when kindness, not indifference, reduced her to tears.

'There you go! You'll be all right now, Miss?' the lad looked anxious and patted her shoulder with a hand more accustomed to soothing horses than women. 'Have a good rest now.'

'I will! Thanks!' she said shakily as he turned away and she realized it would be insulting to offer him anything.

The receptionist took over.

'Mr Torrance said you had had a long day and would have to wait for him,' she said. 'We're not full this time of year—would you like to use one of the bedrooms to freshen up a bit before dinner?'

'Could I? That would be wonderful . . . I can manage with just the little case,' Imogen said, picking it up.

The girl showed her to a small, warm room at the end of the first floor. There was no bathroom but the shower cabinet looked inviting. With a car journey of unknown length still ahead, it seemed unwise to change her travelling clothes but a shower, fresh undies and completely new make-up did wonders for her morale.

She went down for dinner feeling more optimistic and was able to return the smiles from the receptionist and the waiter, and to enjoy the soup, roast beef and Yorkshire pudding, followed by fruit salad and cream that were offered to her. Then she took her book and sat with her coffee by a roaring fire in the lounge.

'Miss Gordon!' the deep, male voice made her jump, uncertain whether she had dozed off or whether it was that the thick carpet had muffled the sound of his tread across the room. 'I am sorry to be so late—I hope you had a comfortable wait.'

'Yes, thank you! Everyone has been very kind and the dinner was excellent!'

'Good! Would it be all right if we collected your luggage and set off straight away then? It's a bad night and we still have some way to go.'

'Of course!' Imogen collected her things wondering where she had heard that voice before and why it was familiar. When she came back to the foyer he was talking to somebody else and, waiting where she could hear the tone of their voices rather than what was said, she realized what was familiar—talking to her he had deliberately slowed and lowered his voice as she had heard salesmen do so often in the office. It was one of the oldest tricks in the book on 'How to get the other person to do what you want' and she knew Roy employed it frequently. She wondered why Bernard Torrance found it necessary.

Arthur's voice, with its wide variety of inflection, but which was always quiet and calm, came back to her memory so clearly. She wondered if the telephone in the flat had ever rung, if he had waited, counting the rings, twenty-nine, thirty . . . when did he give up? It would be . . . what . . . seven or eight o'clock in the morning in Sydney now? Something like that.

'Is this all your luggage?' The deep voice

was back again. 'Let's be on the way then!' He led the way to a Range Rover parked close by. It was still raining and by the time she was in the passenger seat she felt damp. As they left the town he switched on more powerful headlights but the light they threw on the road ahead only intensified the darkness all round them.

'It's very kind of you to come at such short notice,' Bernard said. 'Things were really getting a bit out of hand—Miss Holden explained to you about Helen's accident didn't she?'

'Yes, you must be very concerned for her.'

'She will be well looked after—our relatives are always telling us how much better the medical services are out there—along with everything else. I don't think she was in any hurry to come home anyway! But the children are resentful, not to say stroppy. I have warned them of our approach and hope they will have tidied up a bit!' He sounded less certain of himself.

They had climbed steadily to higher ground, she thought, before he swung across the road and pulled up in front of a heavy, white gate.

'Nearly there,' he said. 'We generally make the passenger open the gates, but on a night like this, in those shoes, I'll let you off!'

As soon as he opened the door all illusion of comfort and safety were blown away. Head down, he ran to the gate, released the catch and swung it open, fastening another catch to hold it open. By the time he got back to the car his coat was dripping. He drove through, got out again and closed the gate behind them.

They were now on a rough, unmade road with water rushing down the drains on either side. There was no sign of habitation. Another gate, and another . . . then suddenly round a bend and slightly below them a group of buildings appeared simply as a weightier part of the overall blackness. They drove through an archway and into a waterlogged yard. The wind and rain beat against the Range Rover making it shake slightly. Half the buildings round them appeared dilapidated, with pieces of sack and plastic flapping wildly. No lights showed.

'I've arrived at "Wuthering Heights"!' Imogen thought, fighting down a rapidly rising panic.

'I did ask them to put the lights on—maybe they've fused again. Stay where you are and I'll open up and bring you a pair of wellies or those shoes will be ruined before you get to the door!' He reached over into the back and found a pair of boots for himself before he got out of the car, then he sloshed to a doorway at the end of a glass porchway and disappeared inside.

In a moment or two, lights came on and he reappeared carrying a pair of green wellingtons.

'You just get yourself in! I'll bring the cases!'

Imogen only wanted to demand to be taken back to Scarborough at once and to forget any idea of working for this man in this place, but it was getting on for eleven o'clock and she doubted that he would take her back straightaway. So she tugged on the gritty boots and scuttled through the door, along a glass covered way and in through the back door.

She found herself in a huge, dimly lit kitchen, warm but untidy. Two cats, curled up by the Aga, ignored her. A door on the far side of the room opened onto a lighted hallway and somebody, somewhere in the depths of the house, was being deafened by a pop group with vocalist.

'Small wonder nobody heard us arrive,' Bernard said, putting her cases down by the door. 'Let me hang your coat here where it will dry off . . . it sounds as though you are going to meet the children tonight after all!'

He led the way across the hall and opened the door through which the sounds were coming. Imogen had only the briefest impression of a boy sprawled on the hearth-rug, a girl with bright, untidy hair sitting reading by the light of a standard lamp and a smaller girl asleep on the sofa with a huge dog, before the dog launched itself towards them like a low-flying missile.

'DOWN!' Bernard's voice was a thunderbolt and the dog dropped within two

120

paces of her, but her thanks were lost in his anger. 'What is that animal doing in here when a visitor is expected . . . and why aren't you all in bed anyway?' and suddenly she was aware only of three pairs of eyes staring at her. She had never realized children could be so hostile.

'Mandy doesn't like going to bed by herself and we didn't want to go until you came in,' the older girl was defiant.

Bernard switched off the music as he enquired whether she had done as he had asked and put clean sheets on Grandma's bed for Miss Gordon.

'I haven't had time,' she said. 'Too much homework to do!'

'Well, I suppose it is something if you have actually done that!' Bernard's eyes were glittering with anger, but he kept his voice low. 'This is my daughter. Phillipa, Miss Gordon, and my son Marcus and the little one is Mandy. It is really too late to get to know them tonight, but I will be home when they get in from school tomorrow!'

'Now, Marcus, get the dog to his kennel and you two girls, upstairs! Mandy you get to bed and Phil, see to those sheets . . . say "good night" as you go!'

'Come on Brute! G'night Miss Gordon!' Marcus took the dog's collar and led him away towards the kitchen.

'G'night!' the two girls went past her unsmiling.

121

'Good-night Phillipa and Amanda!' Imogen hoped she managed a smile herself but she had never felt less welcome.

'Please, sit down for a moment and I'll see that they do get the room ready. Would you like a coffee . . . I need one!'

All she wanted to do was to escape from the horrible children and that dog and shut herself in Grandma's room for the night, but obviously they were going to have to fill in some time so a cup of coffee might help.

'That would be nice . . . should I . . . ?' she hesitated.

'No! I'll do it. Plenty of time for you to find your way round tomorrow,' he said and he left her to pick her way over the scattered shoes and papers to a chair by the fire. Sounds of strife came from upstairs as the two girls argued over which sheets they should use and who was doing the bed anyway. Bernard went up and shooed Mandy to bed. Marcus went quickly and quietly across the hall and upstairs. There were shouts about who was to have the bathroom first and doors banged. But after a time Bernard reappeared with the coffee in large mugs and it grew quiet.

'Sorry about all that,' he said. 'I am sure you can get things better sorted out tomorrow.'

'What time do you all start in the morning?' Imogen asked, thinking that she ought to be given some guidance.

'We all have to be away by quarter to

eight—ten to at the latest,' he said. 'So I hope you are an early riser! I'll drag them all out tomorrow as usual, so you'll hear us moving . . . (I bet I will, Imogen thought) . . . They grab what they want for breakfast and take some biscuits and apples for break-time— fortunately they still have school lunch. They get back about five for tea—we have a rather complicated rota. I expect you will be able to occupy yourself for the day.' He looked rather vaguely at the littered sitting-room. 'But you must be dead beat now. I'll show you your room.'

He led the way upstairs, carrying her cases. The stairs and passages creaked as they do in old houses and the lights seemed to throw more shadows than illumination. Imogen understood why Mandy did not like going up alone.

'That's the bathroom,' he said, indicating a half-open door, 'but your room has its own arrangements.' He pushed open a door at the end of the corridor and stood aside to let her in. 'All yours,' he said putting her cases at the foot of the bed. 'Grandma said it is comfortable. Good-night! See you in the morning!'

Imogen looked round. The dust had settled since Grandma left but the room was pleasantly furnished and decorated country-style and there was a good reading-light by the bed. The bed itself looked lumpy—either the girls had no idea how to make one or they could not be bothered. She stripped it off and started again.

The hanging cupboard contained a lot of clothes belonging to different people as far as she could tell, and most of the drawers were full, but she could leave unpacking until the morning. At least, as Bernard had said, she had her own bathroom, and the water was hot. She had a bath, turned off the lights and went over to the window. At home she always had a last look out at the street light below her, the houses opposite and the plane tree that held on to life so valiantly on the pavement.

Here, she shuddered as she gazed at . . . nothing but darkness. There were no lights anywhere, no difference between the sky and the ground, as if the window had been painted black. But the rain was pattering against it like anxious little fingers asking to be admitted. She drew the curtains close together again and felt her way across the room to the bed. It was cold and she wished she had an old-fashioned hot-water bottle if there were no electric blankets. She wished she had anything to cuddle—but most of all she wanted Arthur!

She turned the light on again and dug a woolly cardigan and a pair of socks out of her case and put them on, then she wrapped herself in a blanket between the sheets.

'And how, dear Maude, how, darling Arthur, would you cope with this little lot?' she asked the dark as she fell asleep.

## CHAPTER EIGHT

Imogen woke unhappily from an uneasy sleep. Her dreams left her immediately but she knew they had not been reassuring and had been played out to a background of howling dogs and children. In a minute she realized that though both dogs and children might have had a part in her dreams they were now a living reality.

The bed was warm at last and she snuggled deeper into it, reluctant to acknowledge that the day had begun—at 6.55. A cup of tea would be very nice, in fact it would be wonderful. It would also, she reckoned, be miraculous if one appeared.

The barking had stopped but the children's voices continued, loudly.

'Well, I tell you there *is* a clean shirt in the airing cupboard—*look* for it!'

'There *isn't* one and I can't wear the one I wore yesterday—it's got paint on the cuff!'

'Pull your sweater sleeve down over it then—it's only paint after all so it doesn't smell!'

'NO!'

'Then find something else to wear . . . I want the bathroom now . . .' Two doors banged and the shouts were muffled.

Imogen got up, washed her hands and face quickly, put on her new jeans and sweater and tied her hair back. A dash of lipstick and quick twirl with the mascara brush was all she had time for this morning. She had no idea what she was supposed to do but felt that she ought to join the fray at some point.

Outside it was still dark and raining. Inside the focus of the battle had moved on from what to wear to where the sugar flakes had gone—there had been a whole packet yesterday. Mandy was in tears because she could not find her ballet shoes *anywhere* and Marcus said that was quite irrelevant—somebody had moved his sports bag so he could not find that either and it was team selection today. None of them took any notice of her at all.

'There is something that looks like a sports bag at the foot of the stairs—I nearly fell over it!' she said to Marcus.

'Oh! Is there?' He went out into the hall. 'That's it!' Without thanks he proceeded to empty it onto the kitchen table, selected what he wanted, added his school books and a couple of apples. 'Hurry up you two! Dad will be in any second now, ready to go!'

'You haven't seen my ballet shoes I suppose?' Mandy asked hopefully.

'They're in your school bag!' Phil shouted at her. 'Why can't you ever find your own things?

126

Get your coat for heaven's sake. You haven't time for breakfast now. I'll cut you a sandwich to eat in the car.' She hacked off two slices of bread, buttered them speedily, smeared them with marmalade and thrust them into Mandy's hand as Bernard came through the back door.

'Ready, you lot?' he said. 'What on earth have you been doing? We'll be late! Hurry!' Suddenly he seemed to remember Imogen's existence. 'Oh! You're up!' he said, 'That's good. Well I have given the dog a run and shut him up in the outside kennel. He'll be all right for the day. . .'

'You can't leave him shut up all day outside like that,' Phil said. 'It's not fair! He's never shut up *all day*!'

'He is sometimes and his kennel is weather proof and he has the run.' There was a dangerous note in Bernard's voice as he glared at his daughter.

'When we are used to each other I am sure it won't be necessary to keep him shut up,' Imogen interposed. 'But until we know each other I think it would be safer.'

Muttering something that sounded very like 'Soppy!' Phil jerked her school bag off the table knocking over the half-full milk bottle that stood too near the edge. The milk flowed happily between the other things scattered over the table and onto the floor. Imogen stepped in swiftly to move books and papers out of the way. It was too late to save the clothes but, as Marcus said, they needed washing anyway.

'I'll get them out of your way, then,' Bernard said and he harried them into the Range Rover. The doors slammed as the engine revved and they roared away from the house in a flurry of water, up the track to the road. Quietness washed softly back behind them and there was absolute silence all through the house except for the milk dripping, drop by drop, onto the floor. Standing, watching it, Imogen began to shake.

Special agents, she recalled from her thriller reading, received training to enable them to withstand deliberate disorientation. She was going to have to manage without, and there was nothing like a cup of tea to start the day, but first of all the milk would have to be mopped up or the dripping would drive her mad.

She went over to the sink to find a cloth, any cloth would do for now. The sink was nearly full of a dark brown liquid that looked thicker than water. Pan handles stuck out of it and a wooden spoon floated. The draining boards either side were cluttered with dirty dishes. As the plug was sitting between the taps she wondered what was blocking the waste pipe. What might once have been a dish cloth was a soggy heap on the soap tray. It was difficult not to think about the smell.

Pulling on her rubber gloves she gingerly pulled the pans out of the water and put them on the floor. Several mugs and plates and a jam jar had to be moved before she found the handful of tea bags acting as a plug. She squeezed them out and looked under the sink for the waste bin. It was there all right, with a cord arrangement which opened the lid for you as you opened the door, but at that moment the cord was unnecessary as the bin was so full that paper and tins cascaded over her feet.

She looked up from the mess and round the kitchen, gradually recognizing the greasy horror of the whole room. Two cats appeared from somewhere and stood looking at her hopefully.

'I am surprised you live here,' she said. 'I understood that I was coming to a professional household, a bit neglected maybe, with Grandma having an accident—but this must be the accumulation of years and I just don't know where to begin!' There were tears of despair in her voice.

'Miaooow!' agreed one of the cats.

'Oh get lost! Go and catch your own breakfast!' she said, and to her great surprise both cats left at once. She was immediately sorry as they could have been some sort of company, but she did not try to call them back. Instead she rinsed out the cloth and wiped out the sink. She did not like the idea of using it on the table but it would have to do for a moment. Once the milk was cleared up she put it on the pile of garbage—it would not be used again.

Swiftly and methodically she rinsed and stacked the dirty dishes on one side of the sink and on the table. Then she went through the drawers and cupboards finding new cloths and washing up liquid, did the washing-up, and wiped the table down again.

Recognizing that hunger could be partly responsible for the new low she was reaching she cleared the rest of the things off the table, found herself a clean mug and plate and put the kettle on to boil. There did not seem to be any fruit, a couple of slices of toast and coffee would have to do. The butter, covered with crumbs and drops of marmalade, looked unappetizing. She scraped it clean before she spread her toast and sat down to eat, but her mind was racing.

How was she ever going to get this place cleaned up? They might not mind living in squalor but she certainly was not going to— not even for a day, let alone a month. In London Cathy would have been in the office for some time now, the post would be checked and the papers skimmed for anything relevant and if Don was not in they would have managed to get a quick cup of coffee!

Maybe it would be better to leave right away. There must be some way she could get a taxi back to Scarborough—but she did not want to admit defeat quite so easily and after all she had really only seen the kitchen so far. She had been deliberately forgetting the state the sitting-room had been in the night before.

Leaving her plate and mug in the sink she set off to find the telephone. If she could just talk to Maude for a few minutes she might find something to laugh about.

The sitting-room curtains were still carelessly closed. She drew them back and looked out onto a rain-drenched garden. It was a pleasingly odd mix of orchard and garden. The stone walls supported fan and espalier fruit trees and the beds at their feet seemed to be planted with currant bushes, but in front of the windows there were flower-beds and a lawn with rose bushes. Down in the far corner there was a summer house covered with some climbing plant and a small group of trees. She looked at it for some time, trying to imagine it in the summer.

Then she turned back to the room. It was worse than she thought last night. Mugs and plates with dried remains of food had been left on the floor by the chairs. Papers, shoes and toys lay scattered over floor and furniture. Imogen went round picking up the papers. The one bright point in the room yesterday had been the fire but that was now a heap of dead ash. There was no sign of a telephone.

The dining room was cold and empty, every

surface covered with a film of dust. Out of curiosity she opened the drawers and cupboards and found some very pretty china and good silver. She could not imagine them ever being used, even at Christmas. Again, there was no telephone.

The hall windows on either side of the front door, which seemed to be permanently locked and bolted, looked out onto a gravelled circle screened by a beech hedge but the only approach to the house seemed to be from the rear, through the yard where they had stopped last night.

A cloakroom under the stairs and a small office next to the kitchen were the only other downstairs rooms. The desk in the office was locked, the bookcases contained a collection of books on veterinary practice and professional magazines and the walls were covered with certificates and photographs of animals but the room gave away nothing of its owner's personality. There was a telephone point, but no phone.

Feeling more and more isolated Imogen went up the stairs. The next likely place to find the phone would be the master bedroom and if she was expected to keep the house clean presumably she was allowed to go into it. She pushed the door open cautiously, feeling that she was intruding. Obviously she was going to have to intrude—Bernard was no tidier than his children. There was another telephone point but still no phone.

She looked briefly into the children's rooms and decided they could wait until she felt stronger—the bathroom with its overflowing linen basket seemed more important. Perhaps they thought that if they left them long enough their clothes would wash themselves! Meanwhile if a shouting match was to be avoided tomorrow she had better try to get some of it done.

She went back through the rooms again, from window to window. There was not another house in sight—just fields and moors and the track winding away over the hill into the rain.

Well, if she was going to have to stay she might as well make herself comfortable. She went back to her own room, made her bed and opened her cases. There was another small room opposite hers that seemed to be used as a large storage cupboard. She found an empty case and packed Grandma's things neatly then she ran down to find a duster for the drawers before she put her own things away.

Pushing open the kitchen door she came face to face with Brute and was too frightened to notice anything else.

'How . . . how did you get in?' Her voice shook.

'He came in with me!' A young man was leaning against the Aga warming his hands on a steaming mug of coffee. 'You're not

133

frightened of him are you?'

'Yes *I am*! He was supposed to be shut in his kennel until the others came home.' Imogen did not know which way to move.

'Oh! I'm sorry! I wondered why he was shut up, but I'll put him back before I go! He won't hurt you, you know.'

'I don't know . . . and I don't know who you are either—or what you are doing here!' He was very good-looking with thick, unbelievably dark red hair and blue eyes. He was also very tall and looked very strong.

'Didn't they tell you to expect me?'

'No!'

'Oh dear! No wonder you were frightened. But Torrance probably only told me because we happened to meet. I'm Andy and I work the next farm with my parents. While Helen's away I come over every week-day to see to the horses and just check the place over. They might have bothered to tell you. Now come and sit down and I'll make you a cup of coffee and you can start to get to know Brutus—do you think he would have let me in if I wasn't a friend?' He cleared the things off the rocking-chair by the Aga for her to sit down.

'Sorry! I am a bit out of my depth! Did you say horses? How many? Thank goodness I'm not expected to look after them as well!' She laughed shakily. There was no way she could check up on this young man, except that, as he said, Brutus accepted him, and he seemed

134

kind.

'There are four horses and some ducks and hens round the place,' he said, 'but Helen found homes for all the other animals before she went away.'

'There were two cats in here earlier,' Imogen said.

'You were honoured. They come and go but they don't talk to everybody.'

'Oh dear! I told them to get lost—and they went!'

'They'll be back—and in the meantime I told you you did not have anything to fear from Brutus!'

Imogen looked down and found that the dog had settled with his head against her foot. Tentatively she bent down to stroke him and he responded by sitting up and leaning against her with his huge head on her knee.

'I thought the children said his name was Brute,' she said.

'They shorten everything if they can,' he said. 'Now, unless there is anything else I can do for you I'll put him back in his run and go to the horses.'

'Wouldn't he be all right out now?' she asked remembering how unnecessary Phil had thought it was to shut him up.

'Better to put him in I think. He might not come when you called him yet, and we are in sheep country—the farmers get a bit sensitive about dogs out on their own even if they are not misbehaving!'

'All right! He would have been company, but actually there is so much to do he would probably have got under my feet! As it is I just don't know where to begin . . .'

'Oh, don't worry too much. You're in the country now, where things move slowly, everything takes its own time and you can't hurry it. Just have their tea ready and they probably won't notice the rest!' He eased himself away from the Aga and took their mugs over to the sink.

'What do they have for tea?' Imogen asked suddenly remembering something she had once been told about tea in Yorkshire.

He glanced at the pile of tins still lying by the sink and grinned.

'It looks as though they have had quite a lot of beans,' he said. 'But there is a big freezer along the passage pretty well stocked—I believe sausages and mash with onion gravy is quite popular!'

'I have not really looked yet,' Imogen admitted. 'I'll have to get them to talk it over this evening. By the way—do you know anything about the telephone?' She tried to keep her voice very casual. 'I would like to have a word with my aunt but though I can find the points I have not yet found a phone!'

Andy's expression changed.

'You'll have to ask Torrance about that,' he said after a moment. 'He has a thing about telephones . . . People up here can get very lonely you see and the telephone becomes a sort of social lifeline, but then the bills get rather high . . .

'He'll have hidden it somewhere, but I'm sure he will let you use it if you ask tactfully—without letting on that I told you!'

'Thanks!'

'Why don't you have the radio on?' he suggested. 'Would you like me to ask Mum to come over and see you in a day or two? She's pleased to know there is another woman round!'

'That would be great—I could do with advice.'

'You'll soon find your way round!' he assured her and calling Brutus to heel he pulled on the boots he had left by the door and went out to the horses. She stood watching to see which way he went, wishing she could go with him for company, but she would not be much help with horses and there was no excuse for going out in this weather with all that needed doing in the house. She returned to the puzzle of how to get things organized.

Arthur would like Andy she thought, they would get on well together, but he would not like Bernard. The second thought was really only a continuation of the first, but it surprised her and she wondered why she was so sure. And the trouble with housework she soon discovered was that while it occupied you physically and needed organizing, once organized it left your mind free to roam. Hers roamed far too quickly to Australia.

She sorted the washing and found the washing-machine, which was an unfamiliar make. Somewhere, once, there was probably an instruction book, but to look for it would probably be a waste of time. She put in what looked like a load, set the dials, pressed the button and hoped for the best.

The next three hours she spent simply tidying up. Newspapers, magazines, comics went into three piles. Out at the back she found many large cardboard boxes and selected three, one for each child and as she cleared each surface she dropped things, hopefully, into the appropriate box. She was tempted to add a fourth box for Bernard but thought better of it and took all the mail, opened and unopened, through to the office.

But the only room she actually cleaned was her own. She was rewarded by finding two hot-water bottles in the bathroom cupboard.

At four o'clock, remembering Andy's advice to have tea ready when they came in she went back to the kitchen and realized she was going to have to cope with the Aga. The cats had returned to sit at the base of it. They ignored her.

She lifted the hob covers cautiously. There seemed to be a lot of heat and the oven was hot enough to roast anything, but she decided to stick to the idea of sausages and mash until she had managed to talk to Bernard about what they really liked.

The freezer was well stocked and assuming they only bought the things they liked she took out sausages and peas and beans and found potatoes in a rack close by. Soon after five the table was laid, the tea was ready and there was no sign of Bernard, but she heard the children shouting at each other as they came across the yard.

'Hullo!' Mandy arrived first and stood awkwardly in the doorway. 'Is Daddy home yet?'

'No, dear! But your tea is ready.'

'Smells like sausages! Good-oh—with onion gravy I trust!' Marcus pushed past his sister and dropped his wet coat and bag on the floor.

Phil followed more slowly and stopped, leaning against the door-post, her eyes swept round the kitchen.

'Oh, *hell!*' she said. 'She's gone and tidied up, now we shall never find *anything*. Have you thrown anything away?' she demanded

'Only the filthy dishwater and the garbage under the sink.' Imogen neither looked at the child nor raised her voice, but it was the voice that had controlled the office, meetings on building-sites and on more than one occasion had quietened a heated meeting in the board-room. 'There are three big boxes over there,' she went on, 'and you will find all your books, papers and bits and pieces in them. Nothing was thrown away.' For the first time she turned and looked at her. 'Now I'll dish up the tea.'

Phil tossed her head defiantly, sniffed and went back down the passage. A moment later, her face alight with mischief, she followed Brutus into the kitchen.

'Hullo Brutus old man!' Imogen put down the serving spoon and held out her hand to the dog. 'You pleased to see them home?' The blank astonishment on Phil's face made her want to laugh but she kept her voice steady. 'Andy introduced us this morning and I suggested he might stay out, but Andy was afraid he might go off and get into trouble with sheep, so we left him in—but I have been out and spoken to him a couple of times.'

'He is very friendly really,' Marcus said, while Phil took her place at the table silently. 'And you've met the cats too?'

'They came in, and went out again,' Imogen said, 'until about four o'clock.'

'They must know you are really a cat person then,' Marcus said, 'even if you've not had much to do with them. If you had really disliked them they would have bothered you all day just to be annoying—now they have accepted you.'

'I wondered if they wanted feeding,' Imogen said.

'Oh! We don't feed them much. They are working cats and meant to keep the rats and mice away—but we do give them a few scraps and some milk after tea.'

'I have a lot to learn up here!' Imogen smiled at him and caught a startled look on Phil's face. Was it, she guessed, the first time Phil had heard an adult admit she did not know everything?

'Has Dad been in?' she asked and her voice was less arrogant.

'No. Last night he said he would be in before you, but he must have been held up somewhere. I expect he's busy. Should I keep his tea hot for him or will he have something different?'

'Typical!' Phil sighed and shrugged her shoulders. 'He might at least have rung!'

'Is there a telephone?' Imogen seized the opportunity to clear up this mystery.

'Oh! Has he hidden it again? He says the bills are too high, but I think it is a bit unfair to you to cut you off, specially when then he can't let you know he will be late . . . It's best to put his tea on a plate over a pan of hot water, but keep the gravy separate then it can be poured over boiling when he's here.'

'Can we have peaches and ice-cream?' Mandy asked when she had cleared her plate.

'Yes, of course. After tea you must tell me all the things you really like to eat!' She felt she was making headway.

When Bernard came in, without apology, at 6.30, she was doing the ironing, with Mandy sitting at the kitchen table making out a list of menus.

'You've made quite a clearance here already.' He sounded almost resentful as he leant against the doorpost as Phil had, looking round the room.

'So, that's where she gets her arrogance,' Imogen thought. Aloud she said, 'I have put all the mail on the office table for you and we have saved you some tea—but if you'd like something different I'll get it for you.'

'I'll have whatever's going,' he said. 'Has anyone taken the dog out?'

'I don't think so. Marcus very kindly got the sitting-room fire going and Brutus went out with him to get the wood, but I think that's as far as he has been.'

'All right. I'll take him out afterwards. Hullo, Mandy girl, what are you doing?' Before she could answer Phil burst in.

'Oh! There you are!' she said. 'Imogen was really very concerned when you did not come home when you said you would, and she thought it very odd that the phone was not here! How could you let us know if there was anything wrong—or how could she get help if anything went wrong here? She's not used to living in the country like this you know. I told her not to worry as you were often late!'

Imogen was speechless. She was not sure what score the child was trying to settle with her father, but she certainly did not like being

142

made use of so blatantly.

'I have a great deal of work to do and I often get held up. Did you need the phone?' Bernard asked coldly

'Not today, but I would certainly feel safer if there was one, and I was puzzled by finding two connection points, but no telephone.' Imogen was determined not to be dragged into any conflict between these two. 'I would rather like to call my aunt this evening to tell her I am all right, but I can write and perhaps you would post it for me in the morning.' It seemed that you needed as much diplomacy domestically as you did in an office. Housework was certainly more tiring. She suddenly realized she had been going now for twelve hours without a proper break.

By the time the ironing was finished and the kitchen clear she was ready to drop. At least tonight she could fill the hot-water bottles.

'Are you coming to join us?' Bernard made a belated attempt at hospitality when she went to say good night.

'No thank you! I feel I have had a long day. I think I'll go to bed and write my letter,' she excused herself. 'Good-night, children! See you in the morning! Good-night!' she nodded to Bernard.

'Would you take Mandy up with you? She does not like going alone and she was very late last night!'

'Yes—I'll see her into bed.' They went up

hand in hand. 'I'll come and tuck you in in fifteen minutes,' Imogen said when they got to Mandy's room. When she returned Mandy was sitting up in bed with a book on her knee.

'Will you read to me? Granny did!'

'All right! Just one short story.' By the time they reached the end of Grey Rabbit's adventure with the Wandering Hedgehog the little girl's eyes had closed and she was nearly asleep and so was Imogen.

She went back to her room, showered, set her little travelling alarm and fell into bed. She just managed to finish a note to Maude before she too fell asleep. Her last thought was the one that had been with her all day . . . Arthur!

## CHAPTER NINE

'It's Friday,' she thought, when the alarm woke her next morning. 'I have not been away from the office a week yet . . . Arthur has not been away from England for a week yet . . . but it seems like a lifetime. Only this time last week he was coming back from Finland and we went to the theatre and everything seemed so marvellously right and went so terribly wrong!' She turned her face into her pillow and wondered how she could get through another lonely day. Her longing for him had become a physical ache that travelled right through her

144

being.

She longed to cry, dissolve herself in tears, melt away. But the discipline of years asserted itself. She had always been the one who had had to keep going in the past and now there was nobody to pick her up if she went to pieces. For a start, she thought, as she got up, she would get that telephone put back! It was ridiculous to be pushed back into the days of the pigeon post or a little man with a cleft stick just because Mr Bernard Torrance did not like paying a telephone bill!

She pushed her letter to Maude, unsealed, into the pocket of her jeans, went down to the kitchen and put the kettle on. Apparently they had had sandwiches and cocoa before they went to bed though there were no mugs on the table. She went through to the sitting-room and found, as she expected, that they had been left under the sofa with their plates. It was something that they had bothered with plates, she supposed.

She took them back to the kitchen and made herself a cup of tea. By the time the family came down the table was laid for breakfast, she had found the Aga instruction book and was studying it along with Mandy's list of what they liked.

'I haven't sealed my letter yet,' she said to Bernard. 'Would you give me the telephone number here, please, so that my aunt can ring me if she wants to . . . and I would like the

145

telephone put back, please. Quite frankly I do feel very cut off by myself here all day. I promise not to use it unnecessarily, but I would like to be able to receive calls.' She spoke as though she had no doubt whatever that he would do as she asked.

'Very well—but I don't want to find the children using it to have long gossips with their friends.' He watched her write the number into her letter, took it and put it into his brief case. 'My secretary will find it and post it,' he assured her, 'and I shall be late this evening. I'll eat out. We have another car, by the way, do you think you could take a turn on the school roster?'

'I'm sorry, no! I don't drive,' Imogen said.

'Good grief! I thought all you executive women drove these days! How on earth do you get about?'

'A car is not really necessary in London and somehow I have never got round to learning. You did not say you wanted somebody who could drive.'

'Didn't I? Well, I would have thought it was obvious!'

'Your letter was unusual,' Imogen could not resist saying, 'in that it only stated what you did not want and I fitted all your negative requirements—why don't you like nurses?'

'They are bossy!'

'Oh!' She pondered this odd prejudice for a moment. 'I suppose I have been fortunate in that I really have not had much experience of hospitals and so on but I always think of them as being efficient but gentle people . . .' (and last Monday I would not have survived without one, she added to herself).

'Well, we must be off!'

The children had been considerably quieter and only appeared to have lost three things each this morning, but when they left, the house still seemed unbearably quiet. Imogen went through to the office and touched the telephone gently. She lifted the receiver and listened for a moment to the reassuring dial tone. As she moved round the house she was aware she was listening for Andy and decided to make a start on the kitchen cupboards so that she would not miss him.

He arrived, whistling cheerfully.

'So, how are things with you today?' he asked.

'Improving I think,' she said. 'I've got the telephone back and I get a dialling tone—I wish somebody would ring so that I knew it really worked!'

'If Mum's in when I get back I'll get her to ring you—lunch-time. It's stopped raining, come and meet the horses.'

She ran and got her jacket while he let Brutus out, and went with them through the farm buildings. They looked neglected but the stables were bright and clean. The horses, in loose boxes, looked very big and she stood well

147

back. Andy laughed at her.

'You're a real city girl,' he said. 'What on earth brought you out into the country! They won't hurt you any more than Brutus would. Come on—come and meet Mandy's pony first.' He led her down to the end box, went in and turned the black pony round. 'Now!' He put a piece of carrot in her hand. 'Keep your hand quite flat, this way and he'll take it without hurting you.'

She watched him and then held out her hand. For a moment the pony hesitated, his nostrils fluttering gently, but then he stepped forward and took the carrot carefully and she stroked his neck and for the first time felt the wonderful warmth and strength that flows from horse to man whenever they touch.

'Does Mandy ride him?' she asked. 'He looks awfully big for her! What's he called?'

'This one is Paddy,' Andy said. 'He came from Ireland and he *is* a bit big for her, but he's not very wide and he's very good mannered. She'll grow into him in time.'

He introduced her to the others, Phil's pretty little bay mare, Nancy, and Marcus' brown gelding, Tom, both Yorkshire bred, and finally Helen's sturdy Welsh cob, Jones.

'I'm going to turn them out as it's nice today,' he said. 'They'll get muddy but that can't be helped—it's better than getting bored! I'll come and put them in before dark.'

She held the field gate open while he drove

148

them through, then left him to muck out.

'I'll be in for coffee in about half an hour,' he said.

Back indoors she set to work again, cleaning and cleaning, but the breath of fresh air had done her good and subconsciously an overall plan had formed in her mind. By the end of the month she should leave everything orderly for Helen to come home to.

'If Helen ever does come home!' she found herself thinking a few hours later as the children came in squabbling like alley cats. At least it seemed that Marcus and Mandy were doing the fighting and whether Phil was trying to call them to order or egging them on she was unable to decide. Whatever it was all about, the noise was horrendous and Mandy rushed upstairs, sobbing, to her room.

'Tomorrow must be different—it's Saturday!' Imogen said when they eventually settled down to tea. 'What happens on Saturday?'

'Not a lot!' Phil pushed her food round her plate with her fork and looked bored.

'Homework, and more homework,' Marcus sighed.

'Oh!' Imogen had been hoping that perhaps they went out somewhere and that she might see more of the county, but that seemed unlikely.

'We look after the horses and have a ride,' Mandy said.

'That too!' Marcus agreed.

'Could you teach me to ride?' Imogen asked Phil. The instant effect of the question was amazing! Phil's whole face lit up with delight.

'Would you really like to learn? That would be super! I love teaching people and Mum's horse, Jones, is ever so good and easy to ride, and then we could go out a bit. Dad makes a fuss about us going out on the moors without a grown up, but if you were with us it would be all right!'

'Well, after a while perhaps!' Imogen was a bit nervous that perhaps she had made a rather wild suggestion. 'He may not even like me riding your mother's horse.'

'He wouldn't worry about that!' There was a bitter note in the child's voice and Marcus flung her a warning look and Imogen became more certain that there was more wrong here than just an untidy house, but she kept to the main topic.

'Well, let's hope it is all right with your father,' she said. 'How should we plan the day? Do you like a cooked breakfast on Saturday?'

'What we used to do,' Phil said, 'was to have scrambled egg and tomato for breakfast, then after we had made beds and tidied our rooms we went down to groom the horses and saddle up while Mum did whatever she wanted to do. Then we rode till lunchtime.'

So there had been some sort of order before Helen went away, Imogen thought, but all she said was, 'I'm sure we could manage that all right.'

They were up bright and early in the morning and Bernard had no objection to Imogen riding Jones. He only hoped she would not break anything that would prevent her working. His evening out did not seem to have improved his temper.

When Imogen got down to the stables Mandy and Marcus were already riding round the fields. Nancy, saddled up, was hitched to the fence and Phil was leading Jones out of his box.

'We've let you off the grooming part!' she said with a grin. 'It's hard work at this time of year when they get muddy—Andy helps or I don't think we would ever get them clean. But first you must learn to put his bridle on.'

She was a remarkably clear-headed little instructor. She knew exactly what she was doing, and why, and she had the rare ability to pass on her knowledge easily. She explained the pieces of the bridle and showed Imogen how to slip the bit gently into Jones' mouth and get his ears through the headstall without hurting him, and the art of settling his saddle so that his coat would lie smoothly beneath it.

'Now, to mount!' Once again she gave a clear sequence of instructions and almost before she knew it Imogen was in the saddle. It seemed a long way up! 'Um! You look very nice up there. I thought you would!' Phil stood

151

back and checked that she was comfortable. 'Now, if you will do exactly as I tell you, Jones will understand exactly what you want him to do, and because he has very good manners he will do it.

Imogen did not really believe her but found to her surprise that Phil was quite right—one movement started him and another stopped him. One made him turn right and another left, while a different combination persuaded him backwards. It seemed incredible that he could understand and that she could so easily control his movement.

Phil laughed up at her, promising that later she would be able to make him do far more. She unhitched Nancy and swung lightly into the saddle.

'We'll just take a walk quietly down the track to the road and back again,' she said. 'Keep a good grip with your legs so that he knows you're there and you are in charge.' By the time they got back Imogen was getting the feel of it.

'You really are doing well! Would you like to try a little trot?' Phil asked when they got back to the field. She explained the rhythm of the trot and summoned Marcus and Mandy. 'If we all trot in a circle in this corner of the field first,' she said, 'Jones will keep the right pace.'

It took a few minutes of being jolted but suddenly Imogen felt the rhythm correctly and they ended trotting in line abreast up the field and down again. The children were laughing happily.

'It's a long time since we've done that!' Marcus said. 'We had a formation ride worked out once and did it at a Pony Club event—it was quite hard work with the horses all being different sizes—you'll have to join the team!'

'I think it will be some time before I'm good enough for that!' Imogen said. They walked the horses back to the stable-yard and Phil told her how to dismount. It sounded easy enough but somehow her legs seemed to have got stuck and it was a real effort to swing her right leg over and slide to the ground, and when she did manage it she found she had no 'legs' left. For a moment she clung to Jones' neck and laughed. 'Do you think I'll make it to the house?' she asked.

'You'll soon find the right muscles,' Phil promised her. 'Did you enjoy it and will you have another go tomorrow—that's what matters.'

'Yes! Yes, thank you. I loved it and I would love another go tomorrow.'

She staggered back to the house for a bath, leaving the children to give the horses more exercise. No wonder Arthur was so happy with his horses. If only she could tell him how she was beginning to understand.

The whole house was yielding to her routine. Gradually the polish was returning to the furniture, the shine to the silver and glass and the paintwork lightened in colour as she washed it. Perhaps the most dramatic improvement was when Andy came and helped her clean the windows. In his company she was able to laugh.

His mother, Mary Dalton, came over as he had said she would, and drove her over to Pickering to do some shopping and go to the library. It was raining again, but Mary's only comment was that they were lucky to have had such a mild winter, almost no snow.

Thinking of the long evenings Imogen decided to buy some wool and knit herself a complicated, designer sweater.

'Though it's ages since I knitted anything,' she said. 'I hope you can help if I get stuck!'

'You have adapted amazingly well,' Mary said. 'Don't you miss the city and your friends being close to you?'

'Well, I have only been away from it for the time of a short holiday,' Imogen laughed. She did not explain that the only person who mattered was so many thousand miles away that an extra hundred or so made no difference. 'And it is only for a month!' She had written to all her contacts and was hopeful of some replies soon via Maude.

'Maybe,' Mary said. 'It's just that you have fitted in so well. Getting Phil to teach you to ride was an inspired move. She loves throwing her weight around.'

'Come in for a cup of tea,' Imogen invited

when they got home. The kettle on the end of the Aga was in a perpetually boiling state and she produced the parkin she had made for criticism.

'Very good,' Mary said. 'But, if you can keep the children off it, it really needs keeping in a tin for two weeks before you cut it!'

'I'll have to make some in secret and leave it for them!' because by that time she would be back in London. Surely Maud would ring tonight and tell her there was some news, some hope of a job that would take her to America, or somewhere.

She hurried to lay the table and get the tea started so that she could cast on her new sweater. It was wonderfully peaceful now in the kitchen. She sat in the rocking-chair with Brutus and the cats at her feet and set to work and the skill, long neglected, soon returned to her fingers.

After tea she settled in one of the big chairs by the fire. The children were engrossed in homework and Bernard, home early for a change, was reading—or dozing—opposite. Marcus was in difficulties.

'I suppose,' he asked, 'computer programming is not among your many talents?'

'Uh . . . hu!' Imogen answered absent-mindedly as she concentrated on the fourteenth line of her pattern chart.

'It didn't run in school today and I am

supposed to get it right this evening, but I can't see where it's wrong.' He brought the book over to her as she finished the row and put a tick in the margin.

'Did it run at all . . . where did it get stuck?' she asked.

'Didn't run at all!' he said pushing his hand through his hair.

'Then it's probably something near the beginning, not the semicolon you have missed there to get you out of that loop,' Imogen said as she read it through again. 'Ah! what sort of brackets should you be using in your declaration—square or round?'

'Oh, bother it—I hate programming! It's so finicky!' Marcus sighed. 'They should be square.'

'Are you a computer programmer?' Bernard asked her.

'Not if I can help it!' Imogen assured him. 'I studied computers simply to be able to understand office machinery and so that I would not be blinded by science when I had to deal with slick salesmen!'

'You surprise me! I thought all you efficient executive women worshipped computers.'

'They have their uses, and I admire the cleverness of the people who have perfected the technology behind them . . . but you can't . . . have a love affair with a computer!'

'Horses and animals are much more interesting,' Phil chipped in, closing her books as she spoke. 'I'd much rather be able to make a horse do as I wanted than run a computer.'

'I think I would too!' Imogen smiled at her. 'Come along Mandy, it's story time! Upstairs with you!'

They went off to bed one by one. Imogen was tired herself but fascinated by her knitting and could not resist picking it up again, just to finish one complete pattern.

'Your references were glowing reports of you as an executive secretary,' Bernard said, returning to what she was beginning to feel was an attack. 'They clearly had no idea at all what sort of job you had applied for. Not that it matters as you can obviously carry your efficiency into any field you choose—believe me I am absolutely staggered by the way you have turned this place round in such a short time. But you were doing so well you would probably have ended up with a seat on the board—so why suddenly chuck it all up? Man trouble?'

'Yes!' She was annoyed by the questions. If she was doing her job here well enough why suddenly start asking about the past—but 'man trouble' was a very good way of describing Broadbent, and if that was a satisfactory reason for leaving as far as he was concerned she might as well bear it in mind if she had to answer the question again. 'But I don't think I have really done so much here. It was a bit neglected but it's a big house and was probably much too much for Granma to cope with, plus the children.'

'A bit neglected! It's never been anything but totally neglected since we came here. Helen has never been remotely interested in housework.'

'Well she had a profession and a career!'

'She was supposed to be giving all that up when we had children. The idea was that she would just do locum work to keep her hand in until they were older, but the place was always overflowing with animals. Then this Australian thing came up!'

'But she's coming back when she's better!'

'She will come back to England, but I don't know that she will come back here.'

'Of course she will,' Imogen said. 'The children are here.' She wondered whether she had done too much to the house, if Helen would be resentful rather than pleased, and whether her efficiency would add fuel to the already smouldering domestic situation. 'Perhaps if Helen had kept her career going so that she had more to work for she would have kept the house better?' she suggested.

'I don't know. The house and the children should have been enough for her . . . They seem to be enough for you.'

'But I've only been at it a couple of weeks!' Imogen cried. 'It is all new to me, a challenge. I have no idea how I would feel once the novelty wore off and I shall probably never find out. I hope to have got a job in America or one that will take me travelling by the time I have finished my agreement with you.

And,' she added to herself, 'I must definitely be away before Helen gets back.'

'Oh!' he said. 'I didn't know you had any such plans. If nothing is settled, would you consider staying on up here? Not as a housekeeper. We need a new office manager—for the whole group. We have always had a man before, but there is no reason why a woman could not do the job—and I think you would do it very well!'

'Thank you! It's a surprising offer . . . I mean you do not appear to like career women, or women in authority!'

'Well, you manage to combine efficiency and femininity in the house, I don't see why you can't do it in the office as well.'

'I really can't make a snap decision on a matter like that,' Imogen replied. In some ways it was a tempting offer. It would be a definite job, well paid, and she would have time to look round the north of England, which she still had not seen anything of apart from her outing to Pickering this afternoon and a walk over the moors with Andy and Brutus another day to visit another farm.

'I am sure that you would want whoever took the job to stay,' she said, 'and I still do not really know what Yorkshire looks like. Andy has promised to take some time off and take me for a ride over the moors tomorrow, but even that won't take us far.'

'But I am sure you will enjoy it,' he said. 'And on Monday I have to go to Leeds, but I can keep my visit short. You can come and see the office there and we'll come home by the scenic route. I am sure Mary will give the children their tea.'

Imogen thanked him and escaped to her room. She wondered what the situation really was between him and Helen. The instinctive idea that she should be away before Helen returned was still uppermost in her mind, but, if she accepted, she would not be living here any longer—and that too would change things. She would no longer be in daily contact with the things she was beginning to love.

The largest question mark of all was Bernard himself. Would it be possible to work with him? He seemed very self controlled but she was always aware of a tenseness in him, and she had not been able to work out if it was caused by the stress of his job or by the unhappy state of his marriage—or had the tension caused the stress and the unhappiness.

The little business of the telephone still worried her and his not wanting Helen to have a life of her own. She thought he could become aggressive if things did not go his way.

Arthur could be aggressive too, she thought, but for a different reason. His aggression would always be used to attain something for somebody else and she wished she knew how the fight in the desert was going. She cuddled her hot-water bottle and fell asleep, as she always did, thinking of him. Any problem with Bernard could wait for another day.

## CHAPTER TEN

Bernard was quite extraordinarily polite at breakfast—even the children noticed. He made no reference to their conversation the previous evening, but he passed the marmalade and offered to get her another cup of coffee.

'I wish I could ride with you and Andy, today,' Phil said longingly. It was one of those days sent to reassure you that spring was just around the corner, and Imogen was longing to get out.

'You'll have lots of days, when your mother is home again,' Imogen said cheerfully.

'Yes, Mummy will be home soon, won't she?' There was a great pool of anxiety in Mandy's voice.

'I'm sure we shall hear from her any day now!' Imogen said, suddenly realizing that she was not the only one to be hiding her feelings and waiting for the post or a telephone call. She helped Mandy into her coat and gave her a little hug before she sent her off to school.

As soon as they were gone she went to telephone Mary.

'The reason for this unusual call,' she said lightly, 'is that Bernard wants to take me out on Monday and he said he thought that it you were not already engaged you would be able to have the children to tea and keep them until we got home.'

'Of course, my dear! Are you planning to be very late—they have slept here once or twice.'

'It's kind of you to suggest it, but I don't think that would be necessary. This is not exactly a romantic assignation—he has offered me a job and this trip is to show me what it's like in Leeds and then, perhaps, to come the long way home.'

There was quite a long pause before Mary answered.

'And what do you think of that idea?' she asked.

'I don't know. It's a firm offer of a job which is more than I have anywhere else at present, but it's not the sort of job I really wanted . . . Tell me, do you know what the situation really is between him and Helen—I think they are not absolutely happy.'

'She was very frustrated when she went out, because he would not let her work . . . She did say that if she was offered a job out there she would damn well take it but I think that was more a threat than a promise—because I am

162

sure she would not leave the children and I am sure he would not let them go!'

'It sounds as though I had better get out, quickly!'

'I don't know—you are both the best and the worst thing that could happen to them just now. You have shown him that a career girl can be a good housewife and you may show her that it is not a good idea to take her frustrations out on the house. You are also a very attractive lady and as Bernard always goes for what he wants he *may* be thinking he can let Helen go and have you instead.'

'Well, that's straight talking!' Imogen said. 'But I think he only sees me as an efficient piece of office machinery! I don't think he would be easy to work for.'

'I must say we would be very pleased if you did stay up here. It's been nice getting to know you. But you're old enough to make your own decisions!'

'And I am beginning to feel at home up here! We'll have to see . . . Thanks for your help!' She went swiftly round the house and laid the table ready for tea.

Andy arrived, riding an old grey hunter.

'Not a flashy mount!' he said. 'But sure-footed and steady.'

He saddled Jones for her and they set off side by side up the track to the open moor.

'Now,' he said, 'they like to canter up this slope. Just sit, quiet and tight, Jones will keep

163

with us.' They trotted a few paces and then he let the grey change pace. Imogen held her breath and shut her eyes but managed not to pull on the reins. She felt Jones' stride lengthen and suddenly it was an entirely new sensation, not like anything she had known before. If it had not been for the beat of the hooves she would have thought she was flying. All too soon they reached the crest of the hill and joined a rougher path.

'Oh!' she said, as they reined in. 'I wish we could have gone on for miles!'

'We'll find somewhere to have another go later,' he said. 'Meanwhile you can let the horse pick the way while you enjoy the view. It's all here, the sea, the moors and the sky!'

She was feeling happier, more relaxed and exhilarated at the same time than she had felt since Arthur left and she was grateful for it.

'It's beautiful!' she said.

'I'm glad you like it,' he said and the tone of his voice attracted her attention but when she turned to look at him he had turned his face away.

They rode on, sometimes crossing roads, sometimes riding on them for a short distance. He seemed absolutely sure where he was going and she was content to follow him, soaking up the sights and scents of the country and feeling the sun and wind on her face.

Then at the top of another hill he reined in again and she gasped with astonishment.

There, at the horses' hooves, was a Roman road, the dark grey stones still as they had been laid so long ago.

Imogen slid off Jones and knelt beside the road to touch the stones and looked in both directions.

'I don't believe it!' she said. 'There should be a chariot and a legion along at any moment!'

'Like a number nine bus I suppose!' he laughed and came and knelt beside her letting the horses wander. He was very close to her. 'My mother tells me Torrance has asked you to stay on,' he said. 'Will you?'

'I don't know. I haven't made up my mind yet.'

'Would this help you to make up your mind?' He took her face in his hands and kissed her very gently. His mouth was clean and firm and he smelt wonderfully masculine of fresh air and sunlight and horses. Despite Arthur she felt herself respond to him and, shaken by the response, she backed away from him gently, biting her lip.

'Is there somebody?' he asked.

'Yes, and no!' she said. 'And I can't talk about it.'

'All right!' He let her go and stood up. 'But remember, Torrance is not the only person who would like you to stay here! We'd best ride on.'

He helped her back into the saddle and they

165

rode down the hill to a little country pub for lunch. Inevitably their relationship had changed but it remained unstrained. He did not require immediate answers. He sowed and watered and waited patiently, knowing that nothing lasting can be hurried in the making.

They rode home a different way, cantering short distances where they could and Imogen's confidence grew. If she decided to stay she would have to learn to drive a car as well, she thought, and when they got in she insisted on helping to rub Jones down and get the other horses in.

'It's been a really lovely day, thank you,' she said when the work was finished.

'I enjoyed it too,' Andy said. 'I hope we shall be able to do it again.' He smiled but made no attempt to kiss her again before he mounted the grey and turned for home. She watched him go, trying to decide how she did feel about him. It was odd, for years she had been surrounded by men in the office, none of whom appeared to find her attractive, but suddenly, in a domestic setting, she seemed to have become desirable. She waited until he reached the top of the hill, where he turned to wave, before she went into the house.

The children came in, eager to hear how she had got on. They seemed to have some plan in mind but wanted to discuss it with Mary on Monday and Imogen reckoned she could rely on her to see that nothing too impractical was arranged.

Bernard came home with a letter from Australia.

'Your mother will be home on Tuesday week,' he said. 'She will still have a leg in plaster, but they say she is well enough to travel and she wants to get back to you!'

Imogen looked round at their smiling faces and thought, I shall have to be very careful what I decide to do. They must not be made unhappy if it can be avoided, but if I am exaggerating the trouble between Helen and Bernard perhaps there is no reason why I should not stay.

That night, when she drew back the curtain to look out, the moors were bathed in moonlight and she stood for a moment going over the ride again. Everything was so clear, including Andy's kiss. She wondered, if she really ever accepted the fact that she was not going to see Arthur again, could she find happiness with someone else, or would they always be second best? At present Andy's kiss seemed only to have accentuated her longing for Arthur's.

The weekend rushed past. The children insisted that she rode with them on Saturday and early Sunday so that they could, at Bernard's suggestion, all go to the coast on Sunday afternoon. They went to Robin Hood's Bay and then drove on to Scarborough for tea so that she did not have to cook—and that brought them to Monday, the day Bernard was to show her round his offices, and the day he would expect an answer to his offer. She did not think he would be as patient as Andy.

It felt odd to be in office clothes again, her shoes tight on her feet and her hair coiled neatly at the back of her head.

'Is that how you dress every day in London?' Mandy asked.

'Every working day.' Imogen was very aware of Bernard's appraisal. 'But not Saturdays and Sundays.' She picked up her bag and gloves and went out with them to the Range Rover.

A Royal Mail van was about to pull into their track when they reached the main road.

'I've got a recorded delivery for a Miss Gordon,' the driver called. 'Can you take it or shall I go up to the house?' To his relief Marcus hopped out of the back of the car and went and signed for it. He scrambled back in again and handed a bulky envelope over to Imogen addressed in Maude's neat, feminine handwriting. She thanked him but put the package away in her handbag without any comment. By the feel of it she had got quite a lot of replies from her contacts.

They dropped the children where they could pick up the school bus, then he swung round and they set off on the drive to Leeds. Sitting in the front of the Range Rover gave her a good view of the country and she looked round with interest as they drove through the rich farmland. The A1 was very busy and they did not talk as he concentrated on driving fast but well.

They seemed to come into Leeds quite suddenly. She had been expecting something like York, but this was quite different. This was an industrial city fighting to find a new identity in changing conditions of trade and there was a lot of reconstruction going on.

'Here, we see ourselves as the northern end of the Channel Tunnel!' Bernard told her. He drove into the car park of a cleverly modernized building. 'This is ours.'

'All of it?' she asked.

'We let off the bits we don't want.' He opened the door for her and she saw him in his own setting. This was where he belonged and he seemed to grow taller as he strode down the corridor to his office. She followed, half a pace behind. Coffee was served immediately by his edition of Annette. He introduced Imogen briefly and simply as 'Miss Gordon, from London,' and enquired where his secretary, Janet, was.

'She had to go down to the general office,' the girl replied nervously and he nodded his dismissal.

While they drank their coffee Bernard expanded the information he had already given her. He had gone into partnership in a run-down firm of accountants in Scarborough and brought in a friend of his. Gradually they

169

had aquired the Leeds business and one in Sheffield, and somewhere along the line, he said, they had picked up a marketing consultancy, a firm of architects and a de luxe private nursing home, to which, he said, with a rare flash of humour, they could all retire!

Janet appeared, looking, Imogen could not help thinking, like a puppy that expects to be kicked. Bernard introduced them as before, glanced at the messages she had brought in and got to his feet.

'I am going to give Miss Gordon a brief tour,' he said. 'I'll be back in about twenty minutes to deal with that lot.'

He took her round part of the building, and the telephones, the bustle were all so familiar. She felt her business persona returning and none of the uncertainty she had suffered when she first stood in the kitchen, wondering where to start.

He particularly introduced her to Maurice Higgins, a rotund, good-humoured, older man who sat behind a door labelled 'Administration.'

'Maurice, alas, will be retiring in less than a year now. He looks after all the offices and he will be a hard act to follow!' and Imogen understood that this was the job he was offering her though he made no direct reference to it.

Instead he took her out to lunch and kept the conversation very general and lighthearted as he told her what Leeds had to offer, the visits of the Northern Opera, a top flight swimming-pool, golf clubs, and the airport handy for flying off for holidays. She was being wooed, and she decided to enjoy it.

After lunch he suggested she might like to look round the shopping centre while he did a little work. She agreed and set off in the direction he indicated, but soon found a quiet coffee bar where she could open Maude's envelope in peace.

The contents were more interesting than she had dared hope. Quite a number of Managing Directors were looking for secretaries who were prepared to travel and two wanted to engage someone in England to work mostly in the States.

'These look interesting,' Maude wrote in her covering note. 'But I wish you would stay in England and give your Australian a fair chance!' Imogen put all the letters away with a sigh and went back to meet Bernard, who was like a small boy let out of school early.

'I haven't had an unexpected afternoon off for years,' he said, 'and if anybody deserves a treat you do. Whenever I think of the house now I feel warm and comfortable and I want to get back to it. I don't know how you did it in such a short time.'

'I really enjoyed it,' Imogen said. They were on dangerous ground and she wanted to change the subject. 'Did you choose the house because it was so far out in the country?'

'Well, we needed room for the horses but then there was all the other wildlife Helen constantly collects. When she is there it's like living in a zoo!'

'But that sounds very interesting—different! I am surprised the children never told me about it—didn't they like the animals either?'

'They knew I didn't—they are quite content with the horses and the dog and the cats.' His voice was harsh.

He had avoided the A1 on the way home and she realized suddenly that they were going through Harrogate and heading for Ripon, and all the emotion she had worked so hard to suppress began to stir and force its way into her full consciousness.

'And this is a place of the past if ever there was one,' he was saying. 'There's the cathedral and that's it—unless you count a couple of race meetings a year!'

'Nonsense! It's a beautiful place!' she nearly shouted the words aloud. 'I was here with Arthur only a few weeks ago and I love it and I love him and *I want him!*' Painfully, he had solved part of her dilemma, now she knew for certain that she would not work for him, though she realized it was irrational at that moment to hate him just because he was not Arthur.

She hunted in her bag for her handkerchief, pretended to sneeze and blow her nose before she said, 'It's often difficult to see why a place exists if you don't live there, and I expect it's sometimes difficult to understand it even when you do!' That served to distract him into telling her about some of the odd places he had visited while she regained her self-control.

By the time they stopped for an early dinner she thought she was behaving normally and Bernard still seemed to be enjoying his time out. It went through her mind that Maude would be quite pleased with her—she seemed to be aquiring the art of making men happy to be with her.

The children, when they collected them, were full of plans. Mary was going to help them so that Imogen would not have to do any extra cooking, and they were going to give her a party tea on Sunday. Over their heads Bernard was trying to catch her eye but she avoided him, busying herself with getting them a hot drink to go to bed with.

But at last they were settled and she could not evade his question any longer.

'I have thought it over, very carefully, nearly all day,' she said. 'Seeing your office and understanding how much you have achieved reminded me of what it used to be like and I am flattered that you think I could do Maurice Higgins' job, but I don't think it's what I am looking for. I really do want to spread my wings a bit and go abroad.'

'And you have an offer for that sort of job?'

'Yes—but thank you for your offer and for today.'

'So, you are going to leave us—when?'

'The children seem to have decided that, with their party on Sunday—it's a dreadful day to travel! Would it be all right if I left on Monday?'

He merely nodded. They seemed to have an unspoken agreement that she would not meet Helen.

\* \* \*

Andy looked very unhappy. He had got all the tangles out of Paddy's long black tail at least five minutes ago, but sometimes it is easier to talk if your hands are occupied. He looked across the stable to where she was standing polishing a bridle.

'So you are determined to leave us! Couldn't you get a job up here?'

She did not tell him that one of the suggestions made to her was a job based in Edinburgh, which had tempted her for a moment. But then she had looked at the map and discovered to her surprise that being in Yorkshire did not put you on the borders of Scotland.

'I think it best that I should go,' she said.

'But the Torrances will fight anyway. They always have done and they always will do—it's not your fault!'

'Well if they must fight I would rather they did it without me!' she said. 'But I shall always remember my time up here happily because of you.'

'Then will you write and let me know where you are and how you are getting on?'

'Of course I will!' He's very young still, she thought . . . younger than I am. There must be a nice girl somewhere just round the corner for him.

She went back to the house. She still needed all the time she had left to finish the clean-up she had started—though nothing could enliven the office except somebody using it as a workplace to do the work they enjoyed. She hoped Bernard would give Helen her head, before it was too late.

Bernard stayed out late every night which eased the strain of 'working out her notice', but there was still the weekend to get through and she hoped he was not planning some final assault.

Sunday dawned, cold but bright, and the children had decreed that Andy was to take them all for a ride over the moors. They would have a picnic lunch and leave the coast clear for Mary to drive over and set the tea. Imogen left soup and a cheese salad for Bernard, who said that was fine, he had work to do and he would take the dog for a walk.

It was with very mixed feelings that Imogen mounted Jones for the last time and followed

175

Andy and the children out of the stable-yard, up to the moors. He laughed and joked with them as usual, though most of the time he was slightly ahead and they had strict instructions they were not to pass him. Imogen and Jones brought up the rear of the party.

The picnic spot was on a grassy patch by a swift-running beck, the water coming down by one little fall, sparkling over the stones to fall again down the hill. The horses dipped their muzzles briefly before the children turned them loose to nibble the grass while they ate their sandwiches.

Imogen poured the coffee and handed Andy his cup. For a moment their fingers touched and they looked at each other, then they both turned to look out over the dales to the distant hills. There really was not anything to say, except how beautiful it was. It was still too cold to sit for long.

The children whistled and the horses came back to them. They tightened the girths and remounted to complete the circular ride they had planned and where the track was wider Mandy and Phil fell back to ride alongside her, leaving the 'men' to ride ahead.

'You must find somewhere where you can go on riding,' Phil said as she checked Imogen's position. 'You have learned so fast. It would be an awful shame if you let it all go now.' Imogen was amused at the pride she was taking in her pupil.

'I shall do my best,' she said, 'because I have enjoyed learning very much. Thank you for all your help—you are a very good teacher!'

'I often think I would like to have a riding school—but Dad says there is no money in it!' she sighed. 'But as it is quite easy to be rich and miserable perhaps the important question is can you be poor happily? If you are comfortable I will ask Andy if we can have another canter up here.' And she was gone before Imogen needed to think of any reply.

When they reached home there was a strange car parked alongside Mary's in the yard. The children urged their horses through the gate and clattered over to look at it, speculating on its owner. Imogen halted to wait for Andy to close the gate and turned Jones to follow him to the stable when she heard her name called urgently.

Unbelieving, she twisted round in the saddle, and then the children were startled into silence at the sight of their cool, calm Imogen abandoning her horse to run across the yard, fling herself into the arms of a total stranger and burst into tears.

Mandy said later that Arthur was crying too but Marcus said that was nonsense because men never cried, but he really had not had time to see because Andy called to them very sharply to get into the stable and rub the horses down.

'Imogen, Imogen. Don't you ever do

anything like this running away again!' Arthur held her head close to his shoulder.

'I wasn't really running away—I just had to leave!'

'I know! I've talked to Don and Maude. Only two things matter now. One, that I have got you safe with me and two, that you understand that I know you would never, ever do anything dishonest.'

'But it was my fault that they lost, what, hundreds of thousands, maybe millions in the long-term because I was careless.'

'No! You've got it all wrong, but we'll talk about it later. Just now the children have got a party organized for you—Mary has been telling me what you have achieved here!—and we are going to enjoy it!'

Over tea he gave them a graphic account of finding his friends still just alive by their burned-out truck, miles from their last reported position. He had feared that they would not survive the airlift back to hospital, but they were tough and seemed to be on the mend.

'Actually, they were not really lost,' he said. 'They knew where they were and if they had not had the accident they would have got themselves out all right.' But he would not spoil Helen's stories by talking about the places she had been to.

They played games until Mandy's bedtime, when Mary said it was time she went home.

Andy asked if he could leave his horse in their stable overnight.

'One way or another I think you will be gone by the time I get up in the morning,' he said to Imogen. 'Goodbye and good luck!'

'It's been a lovely day—thank you!' Imogen said. 'Stay well, be happy!'

'I shall just wait for a number nine bus!' he said, kissed her cheek gently and followed his mother to her car.

'You must stay the night,' Bernard was saying to Arthur when she got back to the sitting-room. 'Marcus can have the camp bed in my room and you can have his.'

'I shall miss them all!' Imogen thought suddenly after she tucked the little girl in for the last time. Marcus was taking Brutus out to his kennel and the great dog stopped for her 'Good-night' pat on the head. It was all so different from her first night here.

'It was a very nice party you arranged, thank you,' she said to Phil.

'And all the better for a surprise guest!' Phil replied with a twinkle in her eye. 'Good-night—see you in the morning!' and she ran lightly upstairs.

'Phil has been impressing on me the importance of you keeping up your riding!' Arthur told her solemnly. 'Would you like to do that?'

'Very much!' They were alone in the sitting-room by the fire. Bernard had given Marcus

179

time to get to bed, then he too had said good-night.

Arthur pulled her down on the sofa beside him and held her very close.

'Imogen, don't ever, ever disappear like that again. I was out of my mind when I could not contact you. As soon as I got back to Sydney I tried to telephone you. At first when there was no reply I thought you were just out, so I timed the calls for early morning and late at night—but still no reply, and when I rang the office I got some extraordinary story from Annette that you had upped and left and nobody knew where you were!

'Jenny and Maude were both away—so the only thing I could do was to take the next flight back to England!'

'But your friends . . . ?'

'I could not do anything more for them than the hospital was doing—they were still not in a fit state to talk anyway. I went to your flat and found your landlady had only Maude's address, so I went there. She assured me you were coming south again tomorrow but I wasn't going to risk you just taking off again! If you're going anywhere you're going with me!'

Imogen pushed herself off his shoulder so that she could look at him.

'I beg your pardon,' she said. 'That doesn't sound right to me!'

'I mean I want you to marry me—and come to Australia.'

They were the words she wanted to hear, had dreamed of hearing, yet . . .

'You say you talked to Don and Maude?'

'Yes! Maude told me the whole stupid, sad story—did it never occur to you, any of you, that, if those figures had been taken from your office there was not time for them to be circulated as far as they had been? They had been picked up in Broadbent's own office, by a computer clerk, days before—because they hadn't programmed in any of the security checks you had suggested when the system was set up!

'Now can we forget all that nonsense? Just say you will marry me and we will have all the drive to talk!'

'Yes.'

The rain was pattering on the window again but now it sounded friendly. She had been wrong to suspect Annette. The poor child had probably been scared stiff that they would blame her too! But it was all in the past now and Arthur was safe, here. With a little sigh of thanks she fell asleep.

She wondered, as she said goodbye to Bernard, if she should make any reference to Helen. It seemed unnatural not to.

'I hope Helen will have a safe and happy journey home.'

'You think I should let her have her own practice?'

'Yes!'

'We'll see.' He handed her an envelope with her pay cheque. 'Thank you anyway for all you have done here.' And for the last time she stood and watched the Range Rover drive away, and for the first time the children turned and waved.

'It would be easiest, I think, if we were married in Leicestershire,' Arthur said as they drove south. 'You may find that Maude already has arrangements well in hand!'

'I'm sure we shall—Maude loves weddings!' Imogen said, sliding a little further down into her seat.

'Why don't we let her arrange it and we'll just enjoy it?'

Arthur took her hand and kissed it, finger by finger.

'That's a wonderful idea . . . I'm afraid you may not like the second one quite so much!'

'What is it?'

'I think I shall have to go back to Australia ahead of you!'

'The accident?' she asked.

'Yes. I'm not the only one who is unhappy about it!'

'Gives you time to get the house tidy too?' she suggested with a smile.

'Ah! Now I don't think the wee shack is quite as awful as you might be imagining, but I will have a go at it!' he promised.

It seemed no time at all before Don was leading her down the aisle of the little parish church where several generations of Britlores had been christened, married and buried.

After the service she watched Arthur sign the register.

'And Lady Britlore,' the Rector said. For a moment Imogen made no move and Arthur laughed and put the pen into her hand.

'He means you!' he said. 'Oh, you are going to fit into Australia so well! You had not thought about becoming Lady Britlore at all, had you?'

'No!' Imogen said shakily. 'I was just thinking about marrying you!'

They went out to meet her mother and sister, old Mrs Enderby, who was taking all the credit for bringing them together, and a few close friends they had invited. Don and Jenny had brought Cathy and Annette and somehow, true to form, Roy had got in on the act.

'It was love at first sight,' Mrs Enderby was saying, and overhearing her, the first of the coded messages flashed between Arthur and Imogen.

'It was for me!' Arthur murmured in her ear. 'You blushed, just like you're doing now— and I didn't think there was a woman left who could! I wanted you then—if I could be sure you would be happy!'

'I hope you are still as beautiful!' Imogen retorted wickedly. 'And now I think you're blushing under your beard!'

*       *       *

It was quite dark when, a few weeks later, the tiny plane carrying Imogen on the last stage of her journey circled the homemade airstrip on the edge of the desert. The sky, with an unfamiliar pattern of stars, seemed to stretch for ever, and, looking down, trying to see her new home, Imogen trembled.

'Relax! It's easier than it looks!' The young pilot grinned at her, and put the plane gently down between the flares lit on the ground and Arthur was running to meet her.

'Come,' he said. 'Step into my world!'

We hope you have enjoyed this Large Print book. Other Chivers Press or G.K. Hall & Co. Large Print books are available at your library or directly from the publishers.

For more information about current and forthcoming titles, please call or write, without obligation, to:

Chivers Press Limited
Windsor Bridge Road
Bath BA2 3AX
England
Tel. (01225) 335336

OR

G.K. Hall & Co.
P.O. Box 159
Thorndike, Maine 04986
USA
Tel. (800) 223-2336

All our Large Print titles are designed for easy reading, and all our books are made to last.